THE SHELF

Kay Dick was born in London and spent her childhood in Switzerland. She worked in publishing and broadcasting, as a journalist and as a bookseller, before becoming a full-time writer. Her other novels include *By the Lake*, *Young Man*, *An Affair of Love*, *Sunday*, *Solitaire* and *They*; her nonfiction works are *Pierrot*, *Friends and Friendship* and *Ivy and Stevie*. Kay Dick also reviews regularly in *The Times*, *Punch*, the *Standard* and the *Spectator*. She lives in Brighton and describes her chief recreation as friends.

KAY DICK

THE SHELF

First published in 1984 by Hamish Hamilton Ltd.
First paperback edition published in February 1986 by
GMP Publishers Ltd, P O Box 247, London N15 6RW.

British Library Cataloguing in Publication Data

Dick, Kay
    The Shelf
    I. Title
    823'.914[F]   PR6054.129
    ISBN 0-85449-002-7

Cover art by Mia Buckton
Printed and bound by Billing & Sons Ltd, Worcester

*To Isobel English, Neville Braybrooke
and Francis King*

I did not, my dear Francis, intend to have an affair with her. Some letters were found – three to be exact – under her pillow. They were mentioned at the inquest. Maurice was hardly interested at the time, and neither enquired about them nor requested them. Legally, he had certain rights to them. He was then a sick man, as you know, and died a year later. Her parents wanted nothing to do with the whole business. With their social pretentions (very shaky pretentions, I suspect) and prejudices they felt positively soiled. They had disapproved of the marriage. Catholics though they were – lapsed of course – they were pleased when it broke up.

The letters: you were surprised when I told you I had them. You were even more surprised when I added that they were letters from me. Though, knowing how little that which is unexpected astonishes you, perhaps you were able to accept the coincidence. When neither Maurice nor her parents bothered to claim the letters, they were placed "on the shelf" which, as Thame told me (I will come to him later), is a repository in the Coroner's office for unclaimed papers. How they came back into my possession is the final chapter of my involvement.

When I met your ward for the first time the other day,

and you introduced her as Maurice's daughter, it all came back. Not that it had ever left my memory, rather that, like the letters, I had placed it on a shelf, apart from the general pattern of my life. I knew you had a ward, whom you visited in Switzerland, yet oddly enough it never occurred to me that she was Maurice's daughter, that she was Anne's daughter. I should have remembered that you and Maurice were old Balliol friends, and that your natural generosity would have taken the orphan into your care; probably Maurice's trustees were relieved to hand over to you. I imagine that Anne's parents were glad to be rid of the responsibility.

When you said to the girl (well, young woman in actual fact), "Cassandra was a friend of your father," I did not add, "And of your mother, too," because, as she stood there, slim, radiant with youth, with that luxuriant auburn hair, I caught a whiff of her mother in her, a tang of that instant sensuality.

Funny about Maurice who looked the typical establishment type. Stocky, fair, square-jawed, of goodish county stock, yet, as we know, neurotic as hell, weak, feckless, self-pitying, deceptive in every sense, with his first impression of being a sound, responsible fellow. One who, throughout his life, benefited from the old-boy system, and whose vagaries and failures would always be forgiven, simply because at school he was the popular boy, the decent gamesman. That he had no family left and money enough was a blessing, and that he died before he squandered it is another blessing for your ward, who now can marry that young Swiss lawyer you mentioned she was engaged to, and live happily forever after, without being haunted by the ghosts of her background. She merely knows, you tell me, that both her parents died when she was in her infancy and, unlike us, who knew them, will never speculate or shudder at the thought of them. That is, you, Francis, will speculate, and I will shudder, not with horror, but at the loss.

"She has a look of her mother about her," I said to you when she left us.

2

"I never met the mother," you said. This because, as you explained, you were in Tokyo during their short-lived five-year marriage. You mentioned Anne's suicide, and the letters found under her pillow which you understood were lost.

"Yes," I said. "I know all about it. I'll tell you the whole story some time."

★

I am telling you this not only because your ward is Anne's daughter, and you knew Maurice, but because you and I have, since the time we first met, grown into the habit of mutual confidence. Do you remember that late evening at Florian's in Venice, those years ago? We were both part of the same dinner party and, when the others left, we chatted until more or less driven from those painted panelled rooms. We reached ease of friendship very quickly. Perhaps that ancient and luminous Piazza inspires loving relationships and the exchange of intimacies. It conveys a timelessness, a feeling that for a while one is divorced from the stresses of ordinary living, an illusion that one is going to spend the rest of one's life in that setting. We had progressed to reminiscing about the more light-hearted of our encounters. You mentioned a man we both knew. You said, rather sharply as you do: "I believe you had an affair with him?" I wondered how you knew since I had kept this to myself. "Very brief," I said. Then, because of the prevailing mood, I told you what he had said to me after the sex: "You'd have preferred it if I had been a woman." You, Francis, were not surprised. Since then there is little I have kept from you, although it is perfectly possible for me not to mention some things. I am, in my way, rather discreet about what concerns me deeply, now.

★

When it happened you were, I think, in Zurich, or was it Tokyo then? I cannot recall which. The child was about four years old then. Nearly twenty years ago – the sixties. The "swinging sixties" as they are called. Were they so swinging? I do remember that we were all much merrier than we are now, generally light-hearted in mood. Possibly because we were all younger. And there was something dizzy about the sixties. We gave more parties, entertained more frequently (were we richer?). We dressed smartly, cared about it, and, metaphorically, sang a lot. A Russian walked in space for the first time, and we were dazzled by the magic of it. The Beatles launched themselves with their fringes, secondary-school look and new beat. I cannot, offhand, recall which political party was in office. Labour, I think, or was it the Conservatives, under Macmillan with his "You've never had it so good"? It was all rather jazzy, not unlike the twenties, or what we had been led to think the twenties were like. There was the Profumo scandal – English morality at its most hypocritical. We wore evening dress to the theatre, went to election-night balls at the Savoy. Of course, that was the beginning of the sixties: the mood was a flavour left over from the fifties. Later it was not so jazzy: Vietnam for instance.

I was, at the time, living on my own, after the break-up of a twenty-year relationship. This you know about. For a year, after Sarah and I had parted, I lived in Adrian's house which he had kindly put at my disposal, as he was then on a visiting lectureship in the States. I had about six more months there, and was wondering where I would afterwards live. Adrian had married in the meantime, and was bringing his wife back with him. You had urged me, in letters, to move from London. A total break with old landmarks was your recommendation. I was thinking about it. You might say that I was at a loose end.

It all began with a "fan" letter. A slightly gushing letter about an article I had written on Colette (you'll remember that series by women writers). Usually of course I just send a thank-you-so-kind postcard in reply, but Anne added a postscript telling me she was Maurice's wife. She believed I knew him. Well, of course, I did know him, and I liked him in the sense that to me he had always been charming and often good company. I had not heard from him for some years. All I knew was the hearsay of his attempted suicide, unexpected news since I had thought him too much attached to life. He had no money worries, travelled a great deal, had lots of friends, and did pretty well what he wanted. However, as we know, the general impression of solidity which he gave was false. There was, of course, his homosexuality and his recklessness in this. That despair at some level was there is evident in his trying to kill himself. I was sad that a young man, in his middle thirties, with apparently so much to sustain him, should have been driven to this extremity, and relieved that he had failed to end his life.

Vaguely I remember hearing that friends of his had taken him away for some sort of rehabilitation. I heard nothing further about him. Certainly I did not know he was married, and, in fact, Anne's postscript made me glad that Maurice had, as it were, finally settled down. She mentioned a child (*waiting for the child to sleep I found this old issue and there was your essay*), so it sounded as though all was well.

Naturally I answered this fan letter less formally, sending warm greetings to Maurice. I signed myself by my diminutive, Cass, as known by Maurice. Actually I should have been more alert, because her *I'm Maurice's wife – very vague description* was perhaps a trifle odd.

I am sure you have anticipated the next move, and there was a next move, by return of post, a rather longer letter, telling me that she and Maurice were divorced. She also told me that, as a Roman Catholic, she found it a difficult decision to make. Maurice, as you know, was not R.C.

She did not go into much detail about the marriage – that came later. They met first at the Catholic retreat, where Maurice was taken after he came out of hospital. I assumed that, like many Catholics, Anne occasionally felt the need for some kind of renewal, which explained why she was there at the same time as he.

I am calling it the retreat, dear Francis, our common shorthand for the rather luxurious establishment to which many "creative" – in quotes, dear – Catholics go. For what? Spiritual refreshment? Actually the retreat is a rather pleasant cheap hotel offering both comfortable suites and utilitarian cells: the former for the more honest, the latter for those who wish to prove a point, I mean about regeneration. I am not mocking, because, in fact, I rather approve of such places, and much may result from a short sojourn. We know, do we not, how many novels have been completed in the retreat, which after all has a very good dining-room, a superb library, a printing press, studios for the visual arts, and rather ritzy drawing-rooms where tea can be served to one's guests. I myself have often been such a guest. I believe the house is Pre-Reformation, and was embellished by Henry VIII when he ousted the monks; therefore, when they came back into their own, with doubtless compensatory grants, the buildings, already extensive, were made even grander. Certainly the grounds are beautiful: the art of gardening is one of the greatest creative virtues of the monastic life. Altogether an admirable setting for the completion of a novel or, indeed, for the consummation of a marriage.

For Anne and Maurice the setting was perfect: totally divorced from reality. Surrounded by the benevolence which such a community genuinely reflects, the outcome was almost predictable. Two lonely people, disorientated, the one by his attempted suicide (oh, they are awfully catholic in the retreat – all are welcome, even heretics, especially heretics perhaps, since there is no more promising material than a sinner for a discreetly proselytising priest); the other, as I later discovered, burdened by a feeling of personal inadequacy caused by the end of an unsatisfactory relationship.

★

6

I do not think you know Father Luke, that fisher of creative souls. You have heard of him of course, and, I believe, reviewed some of his publications (printed at the retreat) which are excellent biographical marginalia relating to various nineties literary and artistic personalities who became Catholic converts. One might describe him as a poor man's Father D'Arcy, in the sense that he deals with budding talents and, unlike the Jesuit, is not concerned with their social standing. A man of fine intelligence and deep compassion, radical in his views. I believe he crossed swords with his Superiors about contraception, and, consequently, was temporarily penalised or whatever procedure is designated for lack of discipline. It so happened that, following Anne's second letter, he came to see me. We were in the habit of meeting and corresponding, mostly about the nineties.

A small man, thin, hard-boned, with a touch of those Florentine monks immortalised by quattrocento painters. Certainly, in a fifteenth century Florence Father Luke would have been burned in front of the Palazzo Vecchio. A sublimated homosexual, I suspect, who channels his sexuality into the monastic life where, through his scholarship and subsequent social contacts, he enjoys great freedom of movement, which is why I nickname him the fisher of creative souls. Several of those novels completed at the retreat were due to his spiritual patronage. I know it is relatively easy to assume dormant homosexuality in the celibate priest, and I should not have mentioned this in relation to Father Luke but for a small incident I witnessed. He was showing me the potter's studio where an Italianate youth sat working at his kiln. I was struck by the extraordinary beauty of the youth, and glancing at Father Luke, I surprised on his face a dazed infatuation as he stared at the boy. Our eyes met, and I could swear that he knew I knew there had been desire in his scrutiny. This is perhaps relevant – in a small way – since Father Luke's comprehension of what happened, and his understanding of the people involved, suggests that his compassion is not merely that of a priest.

Naturally I asked him about Maurice and Anne.

"She did wonders for him," he said. That Maurice had been a pain in the neck to the authorities at the retreat Father Luke made plain. His Superiors were none too keen on the retreat being considered "a haven for people with nervous breakdowns". I forbore to mention the several you and I know who treat it as such.

"Of course," he said, sipping at his Marsala (I had discovered this was one of his favourite drinks), "she ought to have stayed with him." Then surprisingly he added, "However with some things what ought to be on one level is not always possible on another."

"You didn't object to the separation then?" I was being delicate.

"Well," he said, "she never asked me to direct her. According to our Constitution we're forbidden to undertake the spiritual direction of women without the express consent of the local Superior."

"Not even should the need be felt by you?"

"Advice, naturally, is, as we say, imparted, in the confessional." Then rather ruefully: "Anyway she had a Jesuit in tow." Rather more sharply: "I daresay she was safe enough in his hands."

"You don't poach on their territory?" I teased him.

"I act in the margin when needed." He made his point.

He went on to tell me that at first he was more concerned with Maurice, and relieved when the marriage took place, thinking that it would settle them both.

"An erroneous and conventional assumption." Father Luke laughed, more I suspect at his spiritual weakness than at general assumptions.

Anne had from time to time been in touch with Father Luke. Mostly to complain of Maurice who, periodically, would try and kidnap the child, usually when he was pissed to the eyeballs. Father Luke had, through Maurice's Catholic friends, managed to exert some calming influence.

"Shall I see her?" I asked, then not waiting for his reply added: "Oh no, I can't, I'm far too busy. I don't think I want to hear all the sordid details of an inappropriate marriage."

8

"And you?" Father Luke was diffident. "Are you managing?"

I was at first flippant. "Admirably! Don't you think I look well?"

"I was truly sorry. It is always sad when something that has been built up over a period comes to an end. I had thought it would last."

"So did I! Indestructible almost!"

"Situations that start themselves, so to say, usually resolve themselves. When the pattern becomes clearer I feel sure this step will be seen – if it isn't already – as a necessary one for your personal development. Those years had a great happiness about them. You must never forget that."

"I'm not likely to. Quite a chunk out of a life. Was it my fault do you think, Father?"

"Nothing so simple, Cass." He touched my hand. "You've an optimistic outward-looking nature, quick to react, spontaneous. You were up against a deeply melancholic temperament, underneath the controlled sophistication. There was an imbalance of personality. Though," he wryly added, "none of us are wholly balanced."

I wanted to ask him why he became a priest. I did not of course. He partly picked up my thought.

"Celibacy is as difficult a relationship as any other you know. It also contains an imbalance." It was his way of telling me that he too had problems, and his way of reducing mine.

"I shall concentrate on my work. They say it's a solace."

"You have many friends." He smiled at me.

"Yes, I have many friends. How lucky I am! Wouldn't you say so, Father Luke?"

"I think that eventually – maybe quite a time ahead – you'll find what you're missing now." He appeared to hesitate. "Meanwhile, you must be careful."

★

Well, of course, I did see Anne. I felt it impolite to refuse her reiterated wish to meet me, and, after all, we are – are we not, dear Francis? – incredibly curious creatures, and I rather wanted to know more about Maurice. So I invited her to dinner, taking the precaution of asking Sophia and her *cavaliere-servente,* Guy. It was useless to invite Bill, Sophia's husband. Apart from the fact that his work as a film producer took him away so often, he could never be relied on to appear, always having several places to go to at the same time. Sophia then, as you know, was enjoying her first taste of literary fame, not that it made her mild. On the contrary, with celebrity, she acquired a new grudge, ever convinced that her publishers were promoting her rivals on their list more assiduously then they did her.

Sophia who had, as you know (poor dear no longer with us), a positive gluttony for gossip, was eager to meet Maurice's wife, whom she had heard about. Their divorce was news to her.

In retrospect, you may ask, did I have a clue to what followed? Well, difficult to be truthful about that. All I can say is that towards the end of the evening I experienced a kind of shudder, which might be described as a presentiment, a vague expectation of some event to come which held danger.

I did not expect Anne to be so physically attractive, though why I should be so surprised I cannot say. Irrelevantly I remember thinking, "Oh yes, you're quite beautiful, though you don't attract me." And indeed she was.

Sophia, phoning me the next morning, raved about her. "To think that that beautiful girl should have been married to that awful queer!" Sophia was, oddly enough, much given to praising beauty in younger women, ever remembering that in her youth she had been able so to describe herself. Even then, in her early fifties, Sophia was not unimpressive, with her striking pointed features, and baleful yet brilliant eyes which inspected one with a disconcerting knowingness. With her slender height and wiry fragility, delicate hands and penetrating voice, she often reminded me of a goshawk about to bate – if I was not careful.

Anne was tallish, slender, gave an impression of frailty, with small breasts, moved well, had a sort of quiet confident grace, with a soft indolent voice – if I may use the adjective to describe sound. What struck one at once was her pallor, a patina which contrasted with the auburn tint of her hair. The face oval-shaped, the mouth reminded me of a greedy child, the nose delicate, the chin obstinate. I remember taking in all these details with a certain clinical assessment, to be startled by the staggeringly sensual eyes, deep-set and hooded, which flashed grey flecked with brown. A courtesan's eyes, used to protect herself and to unsteady the beholder. Startling because her first physical impact was that of shyness, which later one realised was repressed tension. An elegant and sophisticated young woman was the impression conveyed, expensively dressed, make-up used with professional care.

I let Sophia take over, which of course she did with her inevitable rushing at fences.

"My dear," she said, holding on to Anne's hand, "what a dreadful time you've had with Maurice!"

"I've survived it." Anne was cool, which rather dished Sophia, and it was left to Guy to pad in with some tedious anecdote of playing cricket with Maurice. A memory he returned to at dinner, mercilessly launching into his many cricketing adventures, which Sophia firmly put an end to.

I do not know how it happened but somehow our foursome towards the end of dinner broke up into twosomes. Sophia and Anne settled happily over coffee in the sitting-room, while Guy and I were still at the wine downstairs. This was much to Sophia's taste, because, when eventually Guy and I made our way upstairs, it was evident from the purring expression on Sophia's face that she had managed to extract from Anne a few of the grisly matrimonial details she hoped for.

Anne, I thought, looked even paler, not to be wondered at after an hour of Sophia's relentless questioning. As I came into the room she got up quickly and asked me if I

11

had any aspirin because she had a headache. I got the tablets and showed her to the bathroom.

"Poor girl!" exclaimed Sophia. "That's what comes of marrying a queer."

"Don't be silly, darling," said Guy. "I bet she was difficult."

This of course led to a little exchange of insults between the two of them.

I thought I would see if Anne was all right: she had been absent for some time.

"I've just been a trifle sick," she said.

"Would you like to lie down?" I asked conventionally.

"No, no, I'm so happy to be here." She gave me one of her ravishing smiles. "It's marvellous, Cassandra, you know, that we've met at last."

I did not take that one up and led her back to Sophia and Guy.

Returned to Sophia, who automatically claimed her as a protégée, Anne started, without much encouragement, to talk about the wonderful travels she had shared with Maurice – Greece, North Africa, Malta, Corsica.

"Venice?" I flippantly interrupted her travelogue.

"No," she sounded solemn. "Not Venice, I've never been to Venice."

This inspired me, as usual, to express my exorbitant enthusiasm for that luminous city.

"I've only been ill in Venice," wailed Sophia. "It's an unhealthy place."

"I should like it." Anne gave me one of her flashing courtesan's stares. "With Cassandra – as guide."

I felt irritated, and turned my attention to Guy who was berating Sophia about her memory of Venice, reminding her of the pleasure she had known in that city in spite of a "small" attack of tummy trouble.

"Well yes, I suppose I did enjoy myself there," Sophia acquiesced mildly, as she did when faced with a fact.

It was late when Guy decided that he and Sophia should have been somewhere else, and I was annoyed that they did not offer to drop Anne home on their way. I made

12

some more coffee, and civilly rather than warmly extended my welcome. I asked about the child – your ward-to-be.

"She's exactly like Maurice, in looks and temperament. Terribly coy and cunning at the same time."

Anne was, she told me, living in her parents' house, somewhere in Kensington. She was looking about for a flat. It was useful, clearly, to leave the child with the parents, who, she insinuated, were at odds with her. They hated Maurice, disliked the marriage, and disapproved of her life-style.

"Why?" I made my question rough.

For a minute she looked as though she might cry. "When you know me better, Cass, you'll understand I have nothing in common with my family. I've lived away from them for the greater part of my life. I've done everything they most dislike. Married a man they distrusted. Separated, which is against their Church – and mine."

I felt tired. I did not want too much confession. I envied Sophia who had got away.

"I'm boring you," she said. "Forgive me."

I made some gesture of denial.

"I'm finished," she said. "Life is over for me."

"Rubbish!" I exclaimed, then, without reflection, I launched into my little lecture on the need for an optimistic view of life. You know how I carry on, stressing that whatever disastrous events knock one down, renewal is always round the corner. Once on that track I cannot, as you well know, be stopped. I stressed her youth.

"Thirty-three, are you?" I said. "My goodness, all your life before you. You'll fall in love again. One does, you know, just like that." I snapped my fingers.

She was listening intently, rather more than my words warranted. Again I felt the irritation which shadowed this social occasion for me, and then abruptly said I would telephone for a taxi. I held out my hand to her at the door. She ignored the hand, and swiftly, as swiftly as those flashing glances of hers, she kissed me on the mouth.

13

Christ, I thought, she's to be avoided. I locked the front door with an unnecessary firmness.

★

Her thank-you letter was a confession of love.

All my life I searched for love but never found it, she wrote, telling me that "pity" caused her to marry Maurice, and that as he got better she felt some comfort, yet never *any desperate need*.

I was very cross at being indirectly involved, yet there was something in the tone of her letter which made me patient in my reply, although mine was basically a rejection. All rubbish really, I wrote, one just does not fall in love like that, with someone whom one hardly knows. Even as I wrote this, I knew it to be untrue, since have we not all fallen in love at first sight? You yourself told me that with the great love of your life it was first sight on your part, and you a temperate man, not given to rashness. Why I chose to deny this capacity in Anne I do not know – perhaps a panic in myself. I wished her well, reminded her of the child, and stressed how busy I was – more or less true, that. What else could I do, except adopt a vaguely hypocritical stance?

I was indeed busy, trying to finish my novel about my childhood, or, to put it more precisely, my novel about my mother. Not easy to come to terms with the truth of that relationship. Perhaps the only way to do so was to write about it. I have told you a bit about my background. I have often wondered whether I would have been different if I had known my father – or, at least, known more about him. Mother was so incurably a romancer that she changed his looks, roots (English ? Scottish ?), occupation and social status every time I questioned her. It was not that she was incapable of telling the truth, rather that she did not know what truth was. Perhaps something in Anne reminded me of her. I often looked at mother and

14

wondered how I could be her child; physically we were unlike, although other people saw similarities. She was petite, brunette, and the most feminine woman I have ever met. As a child I adored her, and her life-style, before she married my stepfather, was immensely glamorous to my eyes then. I now know that she, and I, were kept by a series of men who must clearly have been rich (at least in credit), since our household could be described as luxurious.

I think those early years were very beneficial to me because there was no self-consciousness about them. Everything must have been made plain, and the society we moved in was evidently a very mixed one, where normal sexual and social taboos did not exist. There must have been an emphasis on sexuality – at least atmospherically – which influenced my instinctive ability to accept the bisexuality of my own nature, and view it as in no way unusual. Reared in such a setting I was thereby saved from excruciating self-questioning, simply because in my mother's world the people did not question gender when applied to love or sex. Consequently, when I was sent to Geneva for my education (this because my stepfather was Swiss, a conservative and puritanical man), I was already perfectly in control of my emotional *ambiance*, able, quite spontaneously, to focus on either sex. I must add that I am glad that, following Geneva, I was sent to a French Lyçcée, thereby avoiding the *apartheid* of an English school for young ladies.

When Anne came along I was grappling with the problem of how to write honestly about the inevitable conflict which arose between mother and myself when I was in my late teens. Whereas, in childhood, I had accepted her every word as truth, I later questioned everything she said, particularly in areas relating to my father. Was it at that stage that I got into the habit of assuming that all women lied – especially women whom I loved? It never occurred to me that men lied, possibly because my relationships with men have been in the mutual *copain* realm, and rarely emotional. So, you see, I was acclimatised to Anne.

Anne wrote again. *It's selfish, isn't it? For all I know your life may be perfectly arranged*. Ruefully I thought of how, as in the case of most people, imperfectly arranged my life was. *Isn't it typical of me to arrive at the wrong time? At least I recognise myself at last*. She was certainly not afraid to express herself.

My reply was curt, less friendly, brief. I ended with a warning: *I want a rest from love. I've had enough*.

She telephoned. I was abrupt, mentioned work piling up (as indeed it always does) as an excuse for not meeting.

Further letters from Anne told me that she had made the child a ward of court because Maurice had attempted – yet again – to kidnap her. *Call me whenever you want to, Cass*, was her postscript, *even if it's midnight*.

This caught me in a happy mood, having just come towards the end of my novel, so I replied, trusting that her Maurice troubles were now over, and, without thinking, added, *See you sometime*.

★

I lunched with Sophia, who was full of news of Anne. She had evidently been sounding out some of Maurice's mates.

"Apparently," Sophia relished the thought, "Anne was unfaithful. She's had loads of lovers."

"I daresay," I said.

"Mind you," Sophia added, "those boys will say anything about a woman."

"Probably true though. She looks . . ." I was going to say "tarnished", yet changed this to, "looks like a cour-tesan."

"That girl?" Sophia sounded shocked. "Elegant, cul-tured. Reserved."

"She told you a lot."

"Only because I asked." Sophia was touching when she gave her her trust. "I think I'll ask her to lunch." Sophia was determined to play lady bountiful.

I did not mention Anne's letters to me. "She'll seduce all your guests."

"Don't be silly, Cass. You're prejudiced."

"Prejudiced?"

"Yes, on Maurice's behalf."

I let it be, yet felt unease. I could well imagine Anne with loads of lovers, running through them with a sort of dispassionate disregard. Why I thought this then I do not know. It was an instinctive feeling I had that she would accept all personable lovers as they sought her out. Maurice, after his breakdown, had turned to her, and she had, more or less immediately, taken him on. My instinct told me that she did not often, if ever, seek out lovers. Had she ever chosen, I wondered. And now, it looked as though she had chosen me, if the intensity of her letters could be taken as valid. Why was I so annoyed then? I wanted no complications in my life at that time. I was busy, and, in a sense, as Anne wrote, my life was, if not perfectly, at least reasonably well arranged.

★

In order to prove to myself that I had a life in which Anne had no place, I telephoned my agent to give him the good news – so I thought – that I was coming to the end of my novel.

"You're two months late with delivery," he said.

"Can't think that matters, when they always take two bloody months to read a manuscript." I was cross at not receiving any congratulatory word from him.

"Well, Cass, yours isn't the only manuscript. And, how much longer are you going to be with it?"

"How do I know? They might enquire about it."

"Just as well they don't, isn't it'? Since you haven't finished." His tone was hateful.

17

"A little interest would be encouraging." And, from you too, I thought.

"Publishers are businessmen," he said.

I nearly exploded. "Where would they be without authors?"

"Let me know when you've finished. Sorry, dear, must run." He put the phone down.

I worked furiously for two days, and then, exhausted, drove to the retreat. Without initially meaning to do so, I found myself telling Father Luke about the problem of Anne. Defiantly I said: "She just does not attract me. Nothing to do with morality, Father Luke. I don't wish to make myself out to be virtuous. She isn't my type."

Father Luke gave me one of his sly looks. "I would call her attractive, sexually. Many have thought so, before Maurice I gather, and probably since."

"Really Father, you are frightfully immoral."

"I think," he ignored my tease, "that if you could get her attitude to you on the right basis you could do a lot for her."

"I'm not a Samaritan, Father. I'm as frail as the next one – perhaps more so."

"I think you could be an enormous help to her. Keep her at a distance, don't let her make inroads on your time. I'll write to her – in general terms. See if she's willing to see me."

"Tell me, Father Luke, why was she here at the same time as Maurice?"

"The end of an undignified relationship. The man continued to harass her. So she came here – for peace."

"Do men always harass her?"

"Probably. In her, passivity and tension go hand in hand. She invites by omission."

"You mean she's dangerous?"

"Vulnerable," he said. "Maurice must be stopped from threatening the child. The marriage was ill-advised, certainly. In a sense it was a heroic act – of Anne's. She did what she could but he was intolerable, and violent,

18

I understand. She has in her a great capacity for love. You must not judge her thoughtlessly."

"Oh, I judge no one." I hastened to affirm. Yet, alas, how often does one judge without the right to do so? "I do not approve of judgements."

"Not even of yourself?" Father Luke scored a point.

★

Why did I go to the retreat, you may well ask, Francis? Well, I suppose curiosity is the basic drive of a writer, and one has a habit of filling in the gaps. Yet it was also, I think, some feeling, as yet not clearly defined, that Anne was a being in distress. I wanted to make Father Luke take the burden off me. Which he did not do. He left it to me. Our motives are so intricately interwoven and difficult to evaluate dispassionately. I had no further letters, a telephone call or two, one asking whether I would be at the luncheon party to which Sophia had invited her. Needless to add I had refused the invitation.

She sounded cheerful on the phone. "I won't worry you, Cass, but remember I love you. I'll come whenever you call." She slipped that in.

I was flippant. "Any midnight – I'll remember," I said.

Sophia told me that Anne had charmed all her male guests who had tried to date her. "She looked radiant," Sophia added. "I told her to forget all about Maurice and that horror and enjoy herself. She said she would. You've no idea what she endured with him. He constantly accused her of sleeping around, yet didn't want to sleep with her himself."

"Well," I could not resist, "Sophia dear, he gave her a child."

"Oh, that's typical of homos. They want a child – in their own image – but they don't want the woman. They expect her to remain pure and unsullied." Then indignantly: "Those ghastly mates of Maurice – they talk about her as though she were a nymphomaniac."

"Nymphomaniacs go hunting for men. I don't think Anne hunts. She is just available."

"Really, Cass, I thought you liked her."

"I don't know her as well as you do, Sophia dear. She's not my protégée."

"She looked as though she was in love. I told her so." Sophia, in spite of her surface cynicism, was rather tender-hearted. "She didn't deny it." Then, wicked as usual, added: "I thought you liked beautiful women, Cass. Were you turned down?"

Strange was it not, Francis, how often our dear Sophia failed to see what was under her nose. Perhaps because so frequently she saw so much that never was. It was this that made us so fond of her.

★

Have I spun out the preliminaries too much? They are all part of the story. As I write to you now, they come back to me as relevant, yet who is to say that I am not using these details for some dim craving for self-justification? There was no doubt that Anne had succeeded in arresting attention. On the one hand I wanted no complication in my life. I was trying to simplify it. Yet on the other hand, curiosity was subtly roused, even though it was, at that initial stage, a dormant element about which I was only aware when my mind strayed towards it. And, of course, one must admit that it is always slightly flattering when someone, not unattractive, admits to being in love with one. Even if one has no intention of responding, one is far too human not to feel rather pleased. Horrid to admit this; it's a gratification to know that one could if one wanted. I believe Americans call it "taking a rain-check". Rather exciting to have such a counter in one's pocket, rather like a gambler with a last lucky *jeton*. Thinking about it now, with no such *jetons* in my pocket, I am quite envious of the person I was those years ago.

★

If I had not gone to that cocktail party at the French Embassy, I would probably not be telling you all this. A rather delightful party, literary in content, celebrating some significant translation of whose work I have now forgotten. Lots of our pals were there, and quite a number of folk who are not our pals. The deliciously witty Enid Starkie was there, a trifle tight, yet vibrating with life and fantasy. I found myself leaving with old Jawbones and, before I knew what was happening, agreed to have dinner with her. Which, if I had been entirely sober, I certainly would not have done, because, surely she is one of the most incredible bores. Flat-footed to boot! Indeed, as I sobered up over dinner there she was, old Jawbones, going on about all the people she had cut out of her life because of their failure to recognise that her stupendously banal books were masterpieces. There she sat, facing me with her tales of woe, her tales of achievement (she really has mastered the art of self-deception), her rummaging for information on the "who's in, who's out" variation. I knew my expression was glazed.

Jawbones swallowed her trifle, and eyed me beadily.

"You know, I'm on your side. I mean over your break-up."

I stared at a blob of jam stuck to her upper lip. "It's not a question of sides. You can be matey with both. Lovely that! You get a long view on the problem."

"I do think," she stressed the "do", "that you've been awfully brave. Not a word of complaint. I'd have hit the roof."

"Why?" I was snappish.

"Well, my dear – of course it's not a relationship I understand, you understand – but after all those years to throw you out."

"Not quite. Let's be just. I walked out."

"Really! I'd heard differently."

"One always does. One of the delights of having friends."

"Do you, do you mind terribly?" She was anxious to appear sympathetic.

"I miss the rows, you know." I knew this would upset her. "And the midnight feasts of going over things, and," I let my enthusiasm soar, "the attacks on my character and the way I never throw away old shoes. Nobody criticises me now. I don't know how I bear it."

"Is it always like that?" Jawbones had a literal mind. "In such relationships?"

"I believe it varies. I've only my experience to go by. My advice to you," I was enjoying myself, "is never, never indulge in such a fashion."

"Oh, nothing like that about me!" She puffed herself out. "I hope you don't think so?"

I looked at her with cool distaste. "No, I'm sure you're quite safe."

At coffee stage old Jawbones was spouting inexorably on about the number of books she was at the moment composing on her typewriter. Flooding the market with remainders, I thought! What was I working on? Oh this and that, I modestly replied. She was – she spoke with a consciousness of virtue – going straight home (it was about ten-thirty) to write another five thousand words. What was I going to do with the rest of the evening?

"Well," I said, "let's have some more coffee. I'll tell you what I'm going to do. I'm going to have a love affair."

Jawbones opened her mouth as I got up and went to the telephone. My message was simple when Anne answered the call. I mentioned a coffee bar not far from the restaurant. "I'll be there until eleven-thirty," I said.

"And that's that – all set up," I said to Jawbones as I poured out more coffee. She glared at me as though I was mad, and, swallowing her coffee, stalked out of the restaurant, banging her thighs with her briefcase.

Within half an hour Anne found me at the coffee bar. "Hello," she said. "I knew you'd call."

"I didn't intend to." I made my point.

"You had to, because I wanted you to."

22

She looked, as Sophia described, radiant. Then, expert in seduction, she turned her courtesan's eyes fully on me, flashing those grey flecked-with-brown pupils at me, flooding me with sexual desire.

"You understand," I said. "This is merely lust."

"I understand everything," she replied.

Certainly sexually she understood everything, and by this I do not mean that she was given to exorbitant display or unnecessary invention. I mean that she immersed me in a whirlpool of eroticism merely with her physical presence, which claimed response as a long-awaited luxury. I was astonished at my surprise. I had not expected this exultant sensuality, nor had I expected I would feel so much pleasure in her. As I write there comes to me the anticipatory *frisson* which she always roused, and I can see and almost feel that elegantly boned body, the white skin rendered more acute by the auburn hair. And the habit she had of suddenly opening her eyes and smothering me in their brilliant aura. That memorable line of MacNeice comes to mind: *I shall remember you in bed with bright eyes*.

Indeed, Francis dear, I think you will agree that it is right and renewing to remember acts of love because, in the relative brevity of our lives, there is not time enough for loving. Until I brought myself back to recall that exuberant pleasure, I had almost forgotten about it, placed it, as I said, on the shelf, somewhere in my memory. One should be less mean with one's memory of love, bring it out now and then, let it glow inside one as a positive element of experience to be cherished and to be grateful for. It is all too easy in troubled and preoccupied times to forget the blessings.

Her silence in love was not passivity, rather an all-embracing caress. It was I who spoke first. "Well," I said not unkindly, "you've got what you wanted."

"Not yet," she replied. "I want far more than this."

I eased myself away from her.

"You don't believe me, do you?" she said. "You think this for me is just another. . ."

I butted in. "Experiment?"

"I could hate you when you say things like that."

"Perhaps you should." I was back on my not-wanting-to-be-involved barricade.

She ran a finger over my lips. "What do you think I am?" Her voice was dreamy.

"Oh beautiful," I smiled. "Tell me what you are."

"You won't believe a word I say. You've set your mind against me because I've flung myself at you, been totally honest with you." Her hands on my skin were fire.

"I'll believe anything you care to tell me – even the lies," I mumbled.

She came closer. "I don't lie to you, Cass. When will you realise that?" Then she scored a hit. "Have you been so much lied to?"

"Oh, now and then. I'm sort of immune to lies, yet always happy to receive more."

Then, because her question about lies filled me with fury at the memory of lies I had suffered from in the past, I felt brutal towards her.

"Tell me, a passing interest." My tone was no longer kind. "Women? Am I an exception or one of many?"

"Do you have to ask? Aren't you expert enough to tell?" She was angry.

"You seem experienced enough." I made it insulting.

"How long are you going on whipping yourself for your past? I hate your past. Leave me out of it." She gave me one of her wicked smiles. "Exception you are. Dangerous that! You may be setting a trend. I've become addicted." Her mouth found mine. "You've revealed me to myself – for the first time."

I drew away a little. Her intensity unsettled me.

"Do you want me to go?"

"No hurry," I said. "The lies can wait."

I was getting restless, aware as I was of her power. "What do you want of me?" I asked.

"Am I here because I want something out of you like a girl going out with a rich man? I need your love. Nothing more, nothing less. But that's impossible."

Later on, when I mumbled something about driving her home, she told me to sleep, said she would easily pick up a taxi.

★

The next day I played about with the idea of telephoning Father Luke to tell him that really he should not have faith in human beings – better stick to God – then remembered that he was making a sojourn to some Gloucestershire enclosed order. I thought of joining him. I saw old Jawbones, swaying along with her briefcase towards the tube, work-bound no doubt. I stopped myself boasting that I had just emerged from a wonderfully wanton adventure. I spent some time working in the garden, which is for me often a way of quietening uneasiness, reflecting, as I did so, that this was not my garden, but Adrian's, and that my care of it would be limited. I wondered how the garden I had left a year ago was faring. Caught up with the familiar items of my life, I told myself that the episode of Anne had been what is vulgarly termed "a one-night stand". At that stage, I half resolved not to become more committed to Anne, hardly taking into account that I was, *faute de mieux*. I was, clearly, behaving badly, and consequently in a troubled state, while yet permeated with total recall of Anne. I had never before so reluctantly accepted a love affair, nor told myself that this was not appropriate to my circumstances.

I need hardly add that I received the now inevitable letter (silent in the act of love, Anne needed to express herself retrospectively) which was, if over-passionate, rather touching. I could not be dismissive, so telephoned and invited her to lunch. Her immediate reply puzzled me.

"I warn you I hate broad daylight."

"Make it dinner then," I said.

This dislike of daylight, if true, rather interested me. I linked it with the label of courtesan I had mentally assigned to her. "My cultivated courtesan" in fact was my full nickname, because she was very literate. Brought up in France, in a convent, she was extremely well read. Altogether she was, in a general sense, a cultured person with a particular taste for music and opera.

Sophia telephoned. "My dear, who do you think I've had sleeping in my spare room? Maurice."

I became alert yet avoided instant interest with an indifferent: "Really!"

He had arrived, Sophia said, drunk at her house, and was doubtless made even more so by Bill and Guy who poured more drink into him. Apparently he had heard that Sophia had taken Anne under her wing (I laughed to myself at that one), and wanted, as he screamed, "To put the record straight." Anne, according to him, was unfit to be in charge of his child, which, as Sophia pointed out, was a very odd statement coming from him.

"I told him, 'with your boys and your drinking, you're a disgrace.' "

"She sleeps around, always has," he had told Sophia. "Run through dozens of lovers – all rich men. And she's frigid."

Sophia, I gather, had gone for him, so much so that Bill and Guy started to defend Maurice, and Sophia found herself screaming at the three of them. Then Maurice collapsed, and was shoved into the spare room. Sophia lectured him again in the morning. He was sullen. All he repeated was that Anne was "unfit" to be the mother of his child.

"It's her child too," Sophia had pointed out. "And she's better able than you to bring her up."

Sophia intended to warn Anne that Maurice was on the rampage again. "Well," Sophia continued, "all I say is that no woman should marry a homo. They're eaten up with vanity. If they have a child they think the birth was all their own work. She needs protection."

"Not to worry, Sophia," I said. "Anne is perfectly able to look after herself. After all, she can have Maurice legally stopped from annoying her."

"But," Sophia was on her hobby-horse again. "Just typical of that breed always to accuse the woman of being sexually rabid. I told him – in no uncertain terms – that it was perfectly disgusting to talk about that sweet girl in such a filthy way. I watched her with my male guests at that luncheon you didn't come to. Not one flirtatious glance. I can tell you there was one man there who much fancied her, but he got the brush off."

"It's her technique – the seasoned *allumeuse*." I couldn't resist teasing Sophia.

"Really, Cass, you are odd about Anne. She's charming."

"Oh, full of charm, I'll grant you that, Sophia."

"It's so difficult for a woman," Sophia went on. "This is such a man's world."

★

I though I would use my dinner date with Anne to get some facts clear. Heads turned in her direction when she walked in. She certainly had a power to arrest attention. Almost surreptitiously she brushed my mouth with her lips. In dress she had tremendous style; she was, overall, as one might say, "easy on the eye".

"Why don't you like the full light of day?" I asked.

"But I adore the sun. What makes you think I don't? I can't imagine anything more exhilarating than to lie full length in sun – sand, sea, the lot – with you, darling."

I let that contradiction pass. Then, almost to punish her, told her about Maurice's visit to Sophia and his accusations.

"He's such a bore. Let's not talk about him. Why waste our time with Maurice?"

I noticed she drank very little and did not smoke. I made myself impervious to her eyes. "What about all your rich lovers?"

She gave me a mocking look. "Can I help it if they were rich?"

27

"Well, I'm not." I was almost self-satisfied.

She sighed as though she were dealing with a fractious infant. "You want the whole list?"

"That might take more time than we have," I said nastily.

She ignored my tone. "Before Maurice? Well, darling, there was Roberto – such a silly name! We lived in Fiesole. I was nineteen. My first, as they say."

"You started late," I said.

"Darling, please," she put her hand on mine for a moment. "We toured the Continent and North Africa. He became violent. Went berserk. Since then I haven't been able to sleep without taking pills."

"Why did he go berserk? What did you do to him?"

"If you're going to doubt everything I say, yet again, I won't tell you anything."

"No, no, don't let me interrupt. And after Roberto?"

"Telling you all this doesn't tell you anything about me." She asked for some mineral water, and swallowed a couple of tablets.

"What are you taking?" You know, Francis, how prudish I am about drugs.

"I'm calming myself down. You're like an inquisitor. I want to tell you everything about myself, but you mustn't, please, pick me up all the time. You imply I'm a liar. I'm not. Oh, Cass, please believe I won't lie to you."

"Why not to me? What makes this so different?"

"I've chosen you, that's what's different."

"O.K. Continue with the life story."

She gave a merry little laugh. "Well, after Roberto, I came back to lick my wounds. Then there was Craig, an American – for a while. I escaped from that, and went to Finland, for a music festival. There I met Erik. Nice enough, but I escaped from him and met Maurice, as you know, at the retreat. He was unhappy. I was unhappy. It seemed reasonable to marry him when he asked me. I thought that if I settled down – *en famille* – I would gain some peace." She laughed again. "Story over."

28

"And in between Roberto and Craig – was it? – and Erik and Maurice?" I insisted.

"Does it matter?" She sounded bored, a trifle impatient. "They all meant nothing to me. None of them did. I had no pleasure in them. I didn't love any of them. I felt pity for Maurice. He was wounded, as I was." She paused. "Now you'll hate me."

"Heavens, why should I hate you for your past? Lots of people are promiscuous."

"I was not promiscuous. I was searching for something true. Something real. Yes, I did enjoy their company, for a while. Yes, they were rich." She gave me another wicked smile. "That helped. We travelled constantly, which is a way of escape. I was escaping all the time." She held my eyes with her own. "And now I'm escaping no longer, and you want to escape."

"Not yet," I said, touched by her tale of rootlessness. "Let's not bother about the future, at least for a few weeks."

★

I took her back with me again, and it continued for several weeks, this impetuous round of sensuality from which I could not break away. Part of me wanted to, and Anne knew this. "So long as you let me love you I try not to mind that you don't love me," she often said. She kept up the flow of letters in which she spread her passion out with an abandon that frightened me. It was, I knew, an impossible situation. Exciting though she was, I felt her to be dangerous in the sense that she threatened my imperfectly arranged life. Yet she never actually suggested any permanent relationship, merely reiterated that she wanted me to come with her to Paris, to Venice. The travel bug was a chronic affliction, clearly, with her. Then there was the child, your ward. It was doubtless convenient that she and the child were living with her parents,

29

although this was understood by her family to be a temporary arrangement. Her parents, as she presented them, wanted to be rid of her and the child. They were, she said, an intrusion on the routine of luncheon and bridge parties. They wished her to settle down, to find some steady man who would take her off their hands. Money was no problem, because Maurice's trustees were generous in their provision for her and the child, and she had some income of her own, inherited from a god-mother. She spoke of getting her own place, yet did nothing practical to bring this about.

Now I realise that all her life she had been guided, arranged for, that she was incapable of making any move herself. Somewhere along the line she had been cut off from personal initiative, a casualty of her own temperament. Possibly this dated back to that Catholic convent youth, taking instruction without protest as a natural sequence of behaviour, which in her case, when her sexuality began to attract, led her simply to a succession of lovers who took over, temporarily at least, her daily life. That she had run away from them all, seeking, as she said, peace, expressed an inner despair which she was incapable of coping with. She had run right back to her Church, to the retreat, following yet another searing association, and fallen in Maurice's path.

Maurice had hid little of his past from her, and, if I am correct, I imagine she was almost as frank about her life to him. They exhibited their scars to each other with a sort of relish, and Maurice's sudden decision that marriage would sort out all his troubles was accepted by her, simply because she wished for that miracle, a fresh start, which none of us can ever experience. She was almost childlike in her belief that redemption was at hand. At first, life with Maurice was not unpleasant. He was recuperating, had frightened himself with his attempted suicide, and believed that marriage would, as it were, re-establish him. Then, according to Anne, he did not bother her sexually, that is apart from the occasion that produced the child. "That was the most pleasant part of my marriage," she said.

30

Furthermore, as we know, Maurice was a delightful companion, when sober, and for a while he did not drink so much. During the latter end of her pregnancy Maurice started drinking again, moderately at first, and when the child was born, he was, for a time, affectionately protective. I never knew precisely how she felt about the child, although, clearly, she was, in some ways, caring enough. She worried a lot about the child, without being specific. It was her fixed conviction that the child was a small version of Maurice, which I think made her less loving, if still maternally conscientious. Maurice, according to Anne, had encouraged the child in all those traits of his which Anne was beginning to dislike. Indifferent to her response, he reverted to his innate homosexual behaviour, at first with a certain discretion, soon to be discarded, bringing his boys home for her to entertain. I think she might have been able to accept that situation, had it not been that with Maurice drink and sex were synonymous. And in drink, as we know, he was insupportable.

Maurice threw her past at her and accused her of "sleeping around", which she denied. "I'd had enough of that boredom. No choice of mine," she added. Then, tired of the lack of even superficial attention from Maurice, who expected her to remain pleasantly welcoming in the background, she allowed herself to be escorted by the various males they came across on their travels, and Maurice immediately assumed she was easy prey. "Far from it," she said. "I can handle men." It was the first time I had heard a sharpish note in her voice. I gained an impression of constant restlessness in both of them. They settled nowhere. Money enabled them to rent villas in Italy, in Greece, in North Africa and elsewhere. One can easily visualise their nomadic lifestyle. Hardly surprising that the child grew up increasingly difficult to handle, outrageously spoilt by Maurice when he fancied himself in the role of father; Anne's attempts at discipline were clearly of very secondary effectiveness.

"So you took on lots of lovers?" I interrupted at this point.

31

"Now and then," she said, contradicting her previous statements. "I didn't take them on. They took me on." She spoke as though all this were of no account.

"So you weren't as frigid as Maurice said?" I was slightly angry. There she lay in my arms, her abandon prodigiously visual.

She brushed her hands through my hair. "How often must I tell you. It wasn't like that at all. I didn't care. I never have. It meant nothing to me, nothing, do you understand, nothing. They used me."

I mumbled disbelief. With my experience of her I found this difficult to credit, yet I also had an intuition that she was not entirely satisfactory to these transient lovers, and could imagine her containing herself within a barrier of contempt.

"I did not respond," she said. "And you" – she showed a certain anger – "how do you remain so determinedly aloof and cut-off?"

★

My practical side told me I must be cautious. There was, after all, my situation of being partly in limbo, living temporarily in Adrian's house, having soon to decide where I would eventually go. Then there was my work. I had finished my novel, at long last, and, rather gleefully, I took it down to my agent's office.

He did not, as I willed him, turn a couple of somersaults with pleasure. He picked it up from his desk and peered unhappily at it.

"Rather short, Cass. They won't like that."

"Cheaper to produce."

"Not at all! Pity you couldn't have made it bulkier."

"A short book cuts down on their reading time."

"They don't read these days." He was in his cynical mood. "They send it out for reports."

"Do you mean to tell me," I was getting angry, "that my editor is going to take some nit-witted paranoic reader's opinion?"

32

"Oh, I daresay he'll get down to looking at it. No good being so impatient, Cass. These things take time."

Time enough, I thought, as I stalked out of his office, for more of Anne.

*

Was I aloof, as Anne said? I was certainly holding back in the sense that I was keeping to myself my life away from Anne, and this she knew. Something, Francis, you once told me crosses my mind. Speaking about a woman you were infatuated with – I believe she was Italian – you remarked that you "wanted to have the intensity of love without the intensity of suffering". Perhaps in what Anne called my aloofness I was trying to avert the latter. Even so, tenderness was creeping in as I began to understand her better. When the make-up wore off her face she often looked as defenceless as a sleeping animal. At such times I was nearly ready to give her the assurances she wished for.

Anne was often quite witty, but she had no sense of humour nor any of those flights of fantasy which I so love in people. I wondered what life would be like with her when one was not making love. This is probably an unfair statement, yet when were we ever strictly fair to our lovers? Fair to our friends, indubitably so, of course. I tried, half-heartedly, as though it were none of my business, to stop her pill-taking habit which was then, I now realise, too addictive to break.

Maurice was again being a nuisance with his obsession about getting the child away from Anne. Why, one wonders, was this so important an objective for him? Some inherited throwback to his establishment background? A belief that being a father would give him some status? He was hardly able to look after a child. He had "reasonable access", and would present himself to take the child out from time to time. When it was impossible to refuse him this, Anne would never know if he would bring the child back. It was a real threat, which at the time I thought she exaggerated.

Sophia waxed indignant about this, and introduced Anne to her favourite lawyer, who was willing to seek some kind of injunction if Anne so instructed him. This she considered and reconsidered and did nothing about. Her inability to make simple, practical decisions irritated me, yet constantly I told myself it was none of my business. Sophia, I might add, had no idea of how well I knew Anne. Anne certainly did not tell her she was seeing so much of me, which, at the time, I put down to her habit of concealment. Now I rather think she was protecting me from Sophia's comments.

She continued to flood me with letters, quickly despatched after a session of love. Was she trying to convince herself, I asked?

"Surely you understand, darling," she explained. "Never before have I written love letters to anyone. There was no one ever I cared enough for – let alone loved. It's a joy for me to write to you. I enjoy reliving it. When I write to you, I'm with you again." She paused. "Why don't you write to me?"

Her question made me feel mean. After all I had received such benefits of pleasure, and not as yet, as she pointed out, said thank-you. Yet I still felt the need for some restraint: restraint by day that is. By day I often felt this whole affair had gone far enough, that I would have to put an end to it, that it had no genuine relevance to my life in general. Made uneasy by her increasing obsession for me, I realised I should not have allowed it to begin, yet I could not bring myself to end it.

★

I telephoned my agent and asked him whether he had heard from my editor.

"Too early yet," he said.

"Hasn't he even acknowledged it?"

"He will, in time."

"What's he bloody well doing?" I asked. "He might have sent a note. Considering how he nagged me to finish it. No manners!"

"He's waiting for his reader's report."

"Why can't he read it? Has he gone blind suddenly? I bet he's on holiday."

"Maybe."

"Couldn't you give him a push?"

"No, not at this stage. We don't want to upset the apple-cart."

"Fuck the apple-cart," I said, slamming down the phone.

I worked some more in the garden and pulled up a fuchsia by mistake in my rage.

The thought of Anne returned. I was beginning to need her presence in my life. Or rather to put it more truly, I could not give up that luxuriously indulgent pleasure she gave me. Although I knew that ultimately she could have no place in my future, I was stranded, almost deliriously so, in an oasis of sensual well-being. Her ardour in sexual love expressed an unbounded timelessness, and caught me in an immortality of sensation which, as I now recollect, gave me an illusion that never before and never again would I know such felicity. It was an outpouring of pent-up, almost saved-up, passion now released in her, and I was – oh yes, let me admit it – the fortunate one to receive all the loving eagerness of her magnificent generosity of love.

★

I remember an occasion when I thought I could make a break from it. An evening when she behaved without her natural sophistication in these matters, and wanted to stay in my bed and sleep through until the morning. I was inordinately angry, and tore off her the sheet which she had rolled about her body as a gesture of staying-put. I got up and looked down at her coldly, thinking, quite clearly, "Well, darling, this is the end of the affair," and said in a tone that brooked no contradiction, "I'm calling you a taxi."

"You're frightened," she said, as she elegantly dressed herself without haste, then went on to chatter about a young man, a distant relative, staying with her parents at the moment.

I never introduced her to any of my friends, with one exception (the dinner with Sophia and Guy also excepted), which was odd really and probably indicative, because, as you know, I am a horribly social creature, and go around all the time presenting my friends to each other, even when they do not wish to be presented. Friends as such she did not have. Her social life with Maurice, and before him, was not of the kind in which friendships are created. That she was eminently introducible was clear from Sophia patronising her, and I have never quite understood why so often I pleaded prior appointments when asked to join Sophia's various luncheon parties given for Anne. Usually it is exciting to meet one's love object in a mixed group, to watch and be aware of the presence of a lover. "I thought you'd be there," she used to say.

Now, I regret my omission. I should have liked to have seen how she behaved with other people. This was an area in which I had no knowledge of her. Only through Sophia's hearsay, which we know was never wholly accurate, did I gain some glimmering. So I lack some very essential facet of Anne. Accusing her of concealment, when she related her past experiences, it was in fact I who was behaving with secrecy, again alien to my nature which, as you know, is, socially at least, pretty extrovert and open. I wonder now whether, unconsciously, I was clutching on to some exotic bloom, fearful lest exposure to the air would kill it.

One night when I had told her to keep away, not of course as crudely as that, I wrote her the first love letter,

36

the first of three. Not, perhaps, a wise thing to do, yet how would any of us fare if we behaved wisely in matters of love? We should soon be left with no love at all.

"Were the parents rude to you?" she asked once, after I had telephoned.

"Why should they be?" I replied, realising that perhaps the cold civility I encountered was a trifle surly.

"They think you're a friend of Maurice. I told them you were. Well, once you were, weren't you?" she explained.

So, the parents connected my name with disquiet, probably thought I was a go-between for Anne and Maurice. I did not like that at all. It suggested some kind of deception on Anne's part. I had been slightly surprised not to have been confronted by Maurice, then reminded myself that Sophia would not have bothered to tell him that her first meeting with Anne had been at my place, because Sophia was under the impression that I was not interested.

★

Can intuition in love be relied on? What makes one suddenly know reciprocation? Or deceit? Some extra-sensory perception? Mentally, I had put aside the detail of the young man, the guest of Anne's parents. A detail that surfaced unexpectedly. Brought on perhaps by the way Anne smiled. That old primitive intuition made me put the question.

"And your young man?"

I meant very little really, yet as I spoke, it became pertinent. A slight tension in her made me alert.

"Oh darling!" She made to touch my cheek.

It was all there in her voice, the admission. Quickly, smiling at her, at least I think I was smiling, I rose from the bed and clothed myself in shirt and slacks.

"Liten to me, please, listen to me."

"I'm listening," I said, throwing my pyjama jacket at her, perching myself on the edge of the bed. I watched her

37

as she hung the jacket about her shoulders. I avoided her hands stretched out to me, and lit a cigarette, because I knew it irritated her when I smoked in bed.

"It doesn't make sense, I know, my going to bed with him, when I love you. But I was angry and depressed. You did push me out the other night. I thought you wouldn't call again."

"My dear," my tone was as dry as I could stress. "It makes perfect sense. Young men have certain charms. I've found that out – now and then."

"I couldn't stop him."

"Come now. You're hardly naive."

"Why won't you see? He crashed into my room. He was rather tight."

"My dear Anne, we've all had to throw a man out of our bedroom at some time or other."

"I told him to go. It was over quickly. It was his last night."

"Really! Something to remember you by. Tell me, just for the record, how do we compare?"

"How can you be so unkind?" She hid her face in her hands. "I needn't have told you. I needn't have told you."

"Not to worry, not to worry," I said. "It's relatively unimportant."

I drew her close to me. Sexual desire, I know, is contagious. When one has it on one's skin it radiates, attracts others. A young man in constant proximity with Anne then, a house guest, could hardly avoid catching the flavour.

"I didn't want a fuss in the house. The parents would have blamed me, accused me of leading him on. You understand? It meant nothing, nothing to me."

"So you've always said." I made it cynical.

Anger in her showed. "How can you be so stupid? Compare? Comparisons don't come into it. Do you keep a record sheet? Tick off attributes? Let's be basic. What does gender matter? You're the one who goes in for comparisons. So, I've been to bed with several men. Not as many as you would chalk up against me. I've told you, simply,

38

that sexually they did not suit. You're grown-up enough to know what I mean. Would you prefer me to lie to you? To prevaricate? Perhaps you would. Some masochistic streak in you. Really, Cass, why can't you accept? You're ungenerous in your mind, towards yourself."

I made some protest: "Better that way surely, than ungenerous to others?"

"Oh!" she shook her head. "I'm on a loosing wicket here, with you. I've always known it, from the start. You're not in love with me."

"Look," I felt ill at ease. "I don't fall in love easily."

"But when you do?" She tried to press me. "No, you won't tell me, will you? That's something you keep to yourself. Something sacred. It's a very unequal relationship ours, isn't it?"

"Anne," I held out my hand. "I'd miss you, in many ways, but I don't, I can't promise more. And, you know," I tried to sound practical, "in the future, this will be merely another episode for you."

"I know it hasn't a future," she said. "But, I don't care. Why do you think I will change? Is this kind of relationship usually regarded as impermanent? You're wrong about me. I know this will go on through the rest of my life, even if you're not there."

I should at that point have been brutal and called it a day. It was weakness in me that I held on to something I was compensating myself for against a greater loss. And, because I did not want to face any more explanations, having known too much in the past, I suggested we went out for a late supper. So are we cowards in such matters.

★

It was oddly coincidental that, when Sophia came to lunch with me the following day, she should choose to lecture me about my past.

39

"I don't know where you intend to go when Adrian returns. You can't stay here. He's bringing back a wife. I must say, Adrian has been clever. I hear she's an heiress."

"Not so!" I disillusioned Sophia. "She's only got a title. No money."

"Still, I bet he'll make the most of that. He always does make the most of everything. Really!" She gave one of her deep sighs. "I don't know how some people do it. You, Cass, were stupid. That American girl. Pots of money. You turned her down."

"I'm intensely impractical about money, Sophia dear, didn't you know? Heaven knows, Sarah told me that often enough for twenty years. Anyway, the American was too young. I prefer adults."

"Well, you'll have to face the facts. You're on your own now. And Adrian comes back soon. Where will you live?"

"I'll fall on my feet."

"You can't expect to live in the style to which you've been accustomed. You don't earn enough." Sophia relished frankness.

"I'll have to earn more. What do you suggest, Sophia?"

"And, Cass, you were very silly. Obstinate and proud. You needn't have left Sarah."

"We won't go into that. That's over. I must concentrate on my beautiful future. Anyway, Sophia, I quite enjoy living alone – I mean, at times."

"And, if you hadn't been so possessive, so unreasonably jealous. And, if I may say so," she assumed an air of righteousness, "strayed so often."

"Please . . ." I tried to stop her.

"We worry about you. Your friends worry about you, Cass. Can't you patch it up even now?"

"Do you believe patching–up solves things?"

"Well, I couldn't live alone," Sophia said. "Though with Bill away so much in his work I am alone. Once, when I told Bill to go, to get out of the house, he sat on the bed and said he was very comfortable thank-you. What could I do?"

40

"What about Guy?"

"Yes, of course, he comes every day. I have to have a man around. It's that terrible childhood of mine. The insecurity of parents hating each other. No one knows how it scarred me. You're lucky, Cass, you've had a lovely childhood. All that glamour and foreign travel. Not like mine. And the lack of money. Quarrelling over every penny. Can you imagine what it's like for four people to live on an ex-naval officer's pension? I couldn't wait to get away. You've been spoilt all your life, Cass."

"Perhaps, in some ways. At least it's made me think that people are rather nice. I have an optimistic view of life, Sophia."

"You won't face reality. If you'd had half my privations, well . . . Your mother never told you, as mine did me, that I was a disappointment to her. I adored my brother but I bullied him from sheer jealousy. Then he was killed at Alamein, and I felt I had wished his death. You expect people to like you, Cass. I never expect people to like me. It took me a long time to feel secure. You've had it easy, Cass."

"I daresay I'll have to make up for that now. Watch me sweat, Sophia."

"And money, Cass? What do you think you can do on your own?"

"I have a wonderful survival kit, all ready for use. And, I can work, you know."

"Authors are paid a pittance."

"You don't do so badly." I thought of Sophia's beautiful house and rather rich lifestyle.

"It's been a struggle, I can tell you. In my youth, I worked from nine until six for fifteen shillings a week in a dreadful office. One meal a day, and tea and toast for supper. I'd write my novels until eleven at night. Pure slavery. I told Bill about those years. Water off a duck's back! I've been as poor as Katherine Mansfield was."

"She always exaggerated."

"It's hard for a woman alone. I had to write. I couldn't possibly be just a wife. I've always felt the need to explain myself, because I've felt so acutely in the wrong. Perhaps you should marry."

"I'll think about it."

"Oh, Cass, I know you present a brave face – so do I! But you won't face facts. Your situation is altered now. A woman alone has no chance in this world."

"That's a bit out-of-date, isn't it? Women do rather well on their own – some of them."

"And you're extravagant. You buy expensive clothes. And your car – you can't expect to run that much longer. If you'd had to scrape and save as I've done, you'd look at things differently. Bill has no idea of money. If it weren't for me, I don't know where we'd be. I begin to think we can't even afford a roof over our heads."

"Oh, I always live, like Wilde, beyond my means."

"Well, you must stop it." Sophia could never recognise a joke. "What are we to do with you? You're an awful worry. It's all very well for a woman like Anne, who has a private income, and will get married again."

"What about me?" I liked teasing Sophia. "Thought you said I could get married?"

"But you, Cass, like women best."

"So do lots of married women. Didn't you know Sophia?"

"Well, yes, and, really, I don't blame them, considering some of the husbands."

"I'll tell you what. If you and all my dear friends stop nagging me, I'll get settled – some time or other."

"You'll have to work very hard, very hard indeed, Cass. You've no discipline."

"You frighten me, Sophia. Now, why don't we start lunch?"

"I must say," Sophia peered about her, "Adrian has collected some very nice things." She inspected a stack of paintings up against a wall.

"Those are mine," I said, which she did not expect.

"And your books? What are you going to do with all your books?"

"Put them on shelves."

"You'll need a big place. That will cost something."

"I'll have a large workroom, put in a bed, and invite you to tea."

"Well, I suppose you know what you're doing."

"Yes, Sophia, I do know. Trying to live again."

★

The next day my agent called telling me to phone my editor.

"Why can't he phone me?"

"He's busy. Now, be a dear, Cass, give him a ring." My agent had a genius for telephone brevity.

I got through, eventually, after being told that the swine was "in conference". I waited for some word of appreciation from him.

"Hello, Cass," he sounded horribly breezy. "About your manuscript. Those first three chapters. They're a bit coagulated."

I could have screamed. "Coagulated?"

"Who's that chap George for instance?"

"There is no George in my novel." I hoped I conveyed my contempt.

"Sorry. No, I see, the Geoffrey character."

The bugger had not read it properly, I thought.

"And," his voice was more and more distasteful to me, "I couldn't get it. Your motivation?"

I controlled myself. "I thought I had made it quite clear." My voice was steely.

"Look, I'm a bit pressed. I'll drop you a note about it." He rang off before I exploded.

I forgot to mention that part of my daily life – my life away from Anne, that is – was concerned with Adrian's new neighbours, who had moved in three months after Adrian left. A family of four noisome morons with whom, over the past nine months, I had fought a running battle. Adrian's terraced house adjoined the next one.

The neighbours threw their furniture about during the early hours of the morning, installed a washing-machine which they used constantly at all hours of day and night, and positively revelled in putting up the sound of their television to an unbearable pitch.

Suffering deep shock from my conversation with my editor, I went almost berserk as the television blared its loudest from next door. I fetched the Hoover, switched it on, and pressed it against the adjoining wall. It was a losing battle as far as I was concerned. I went into the garden and planted some bulbs.

★

One afternoon Anne sprung an odd sort of surprise on me, especially so since usually she was never available during the day – which suited me quite well, and which I put down to her concern to give her daytime to the child. She gave me an address off Jermyn Street. When I arrived she was bubblingly excited. We were standing at the entrance to a block of mansion flats. Here she led me, past a small porter's lodge, opening the door to one of the apartments on the first floor. It consisted of one large room and bathroom. Expensive yet subdued in its accoutrements, with a bottle of champagne and two glasses on a table. Its basic purpose was clear, the bed evident, as in an hotel room. I was furious.

"Your turn to bring someone here, is it?" I was unreasonably rude. "When did you last visit? Recently?"

I faced her with contempt. She sank down on the bed and gave a sigh. I let her be for a few minutes, while I paced the room, reciting aloud an inventory of its contents, and likewise toured the bathroom. "Expensive, oh yes, I can see that. You've been used to style. All very discreet. Nothing flash, nothing jazzy. Is there room-service? Suppose I get hungry?"

"You can order whatever you like." She ignored my temper.

"Perhaps I could order a taxi? Ah yes, there's the phone, conveniently placed by the bed."

"You are wretched," she said quietly. "Wretched at times. Don't you understand? I wanted to invite you. I haven't a place of my own. A hotel wouldn't do for a few hours."

"No, certainly not. A hotel is too public. This is for an afternoon out. Tell me, is tea served?" I became uncouth. "Who brought you here first?"

"Actually" – she smiled faintly – "if you really want or need to know, it was Maurice. Before we were married. He knew it."

"Ah yes, this is where he brought his boys." I was being vulgar. "So it's more or less part of the family pattern, isn't it?"

"Darling, you look like an outraged goose when you're cross." She came towards me. "Why waste this champagne?"

"Provided by the management?" I snapped.

"No, darling. I brought it with me." She handed me a glass, having opened the bottle so softly that I had been unaware of her so doing. "Temper over? Stop behaving like the country cousin."

"Oh well" – I drank – "I've always wondered where the rich fornicated." I waved at the furniture. "Maples or Harrods, do you think?"

"Come here," she said. "Stop being a tourist."

"Only Maurice?" I asked as she laid her hands on me.

"I think so," she teased. "But then you don't care, do you? You don't care at all. This is just happening to you. Nothing to do with your will-power. You remain cool, don't you? Perhaps it isn't you at all that I'm seducing yet again."

Was her life cluttered with such rooms, I asked myself, or rather apartments, from which she would eventually run away? This thought of her near-total rootlessness touched me to tenderness, and I did all I could to erase the memory of my previous bad humour.

45

"It won't always be like this, will it? In rented rooms?" She was not as silent as usual; possibly such rooms stirred unfortunate memories of occasions when chatter had been a way out. "I mean for us. Oh I would like, I would like this to go on for ever. Now don't flinch. I accept. I give in. I demand nothing from you but what you choose to give now."

As we left the porter treated us as though we were residents, with his suave, "Good evening, Madam."

I could not resist. "One doesn't pay on the spot. No, that would be too undignified."

"You're a masochist, Cass," she said. "You have to punish yourself for your pleasures."

"And you?"

"I've had so few that I value them when they come my way."

We were sitting in a nearby bar. She made me feel small-minded, puritanical. I looked at her face. Her eyes steadily held mine.

"I know you don't really want to hear this, although part of you does, for me this is and always will be. Whatever may happen in the future. You can go your own way, as obviously you must. I never thought I would love anyone. It's flowing through me all the time. Please," her face came near mine. "Take it. It's the only gift I can give you. I never could give myself before. I mean all of myself, not only the sex. You don't want me to be serious, do you?"

I spoke truthfully. "I don't know what I want."

That night, without her, I wrote her my second love letter.

★

Shortly after that I lunched with Sophia. I nearly confided in her, yet, thankfully, restrained myself. Sophia, as we know, could never be trusted with confidential matters, although able to understand behaviour and motive as well and as sensitively as anyone. A comprehension and sensibility she kept for her writing.

Instead, I unburdened myself about agents and publishers.

"My dear, agents crawl to publishers!" Sophia was very emphatic. "We authors are just dross to them both. My agent hardly speaks to me ever since I told him he was a bloodsucking vampire. As for my publisher, well, I don't think he can read. All he thinks about is money – like a potato merchant. As for selling me in paperback, he couldn't care less. And, to think that I sweat blood writing for him. I get no sympathy from Bill. They play in the same cricket team. In Bill's eyes, that makes him perfect."

"But you are in paperback," I pointed out.

"Yes, but only because I pushed him to it. All he cares about are those ghastly bestsellers of his."

"You sell quite well, don't you?"

"Yes, I suppose I do. But I don't get my fair share of advertising. They promote that grubby girl who writes about unmarried mothers and that sex-obsessed foreign adulterer. I can tell you, I know what it's like to be neglected."

"But you're not. You're well reviewed, written about, reprinted. What more do you want?"

"And where does it get me? There are times when I wish I were like Anne, with a private income. Which reminds me. Maurice wants Anne back."

"Ridiculous!" I retorted. "They're divorced."

"It's the child. He's mad about that child. He thinks Anne will forgive him if he promises to behave."

"What, no drink? No boys? No racketing about in foreign climes?" A thought struck me. "Do you think Anne would take him back?" After all Sophia knew a different face of Anne.

"I think she'd like a settled life. Most women do. Although I must say it's mostly the woman who gets settled, not the man. She told me she would."

"She told you she wanted a settled life?" I felt indignant.

"Sort of. Those parents of hers are very tedious. It's almost impossible for her to get out. She hardly does, you know."

"Really!" I was interested.

"They ask questions all the time. Who she is seeing. How long she's known them. She's spied on."

"Come off it, Sophia, that's melodrama."

"So you say, but what do you know? She goes to lots of concerts, you know she's very musical. She has an awful trouble getting out in the evenings. They treat her as though she were a juvenile. They resent me, you know. I'm a bad influence. I know Maurice. I introduce her to lots of interesting people. They hate interesting people." Sophia was unaware of her own incongruity. "Guy drove her home from my place once. They wanted to know all about him. She's a prisoner."

I wanted to laugh. "So you think returning to Maurice would solve all Anne's problems?"

"Well, he can be charming."

"But, Sophia, you think him impossible, so you've often said."

"Well, my dear, who is possible? He can provide a background. When he's not drinking, he's presentable enough. We can't all be as independent as you, Cass." Sophia gave me one of her grim smiles.

"I love to think of you, Sophia dear, as a match-maker."

"Mind you, I wouldn't have Maurice, not if you paid me." Blissfully unconscious, as usual, of contradiction.

"Would you," I asked Anne when we next met, "return to Maurice?"

"Are you mad? I've run away from him, and I'm still running from all that. He talked about our getting together again when he last came to take the child out. The idea is sheer terror to me. How could you even ask? Haven't I made plain what I want? What I can't have."

I dropped the subject, yet did wonder whether the possibility existed, and, coward that I was, part of me welcomed the idea of Anne settled again.

Really, Francis, before I knew what was happening, Anne took over my daily life, or rather, let me be more accurate, I was more and more in need of her physical presence. Intoxication is perhaps the right word. So I gave myself up to the delight, a state of rapture which must have communicated itself to others, because everywhere I went people commented on how well I looked, how evidently "on top", as they say, I was. This was put down to my work which also had enjoyed a beneficial stimulus, in that I felt no hesitation in execution, was able as it were to soar along with a prolific ease. In that area of my life Anne was indeed a blessing, and I told her so, not wanting to keep any favour she gave me from her, simply because, so often, she would remark how wounding her presence had been to those who loved her. Wounding by default, because, as she put it, "They expected me to be other than I am."

The Italian had wanted her to remain his flawless mistress with social accomplishments as well as bed. He expected her to command and control his servants, and entertain his guests, to shine when he took her out. When she grew bored with this role, for which of course she was supremely educated in that convent for *jeunes filles bien élevées*, he displayed temper.

"That," she said, "I wasn't having."

She had packed and left. He had followed and brought her back.

"In a way I liked the Italian lifestyle. That's probably why I went back with him."

When it became clear to him that she was sexually bored with him, he, as did Maurice, had accused her of being frigid.

"Though why he didn't realise his failure to please me in bed before, I don't know. He only thought of his own pleasure," she said, then added: "He was tedious in his assumptions."

I gather there was a final mighty explosion when he threatened to kill her, and, by mistake, shot himself in the arm.

"He was melodramatic," she said. "Interesting, cultured in his fashion, but excruciatingly Italian. I left for good."

The American, so she explained, had failed totally to see her as she was. He had come to Europe for life and art, writing plays which no one wanted, and thought that a mistress was an inevitable part of this Grand Tour. She ran away from that one.

"He had no talent, in fact. He cried when I left, more at his own incapacity to please me than for my departure."

The Finn had attracted her because of his music: he was a budding composer.

"All he really wanted was an unpaid housewife."

She was not without money. The godmother who had paid for her education had left her a legacy which, sensibly enough, she had invested.

I asked whom she was escaping from when she went to the retreat.

She brushed this aside rather. "Oh some man who wouldn't take no for an answer."

Father Luke must have got it wrong with his "undignified relationship", although he had added that the man in question continued to harass her.

"You see, I was never allowed to be myself. I was always put into some masculine fantasy. Whatever image they created for me in their lives I temporarily became, at least to them."

"Had you no will-power in all this?" I spoke crossly, not understanding how some people can be so suggestible as to become what others have willed them to be.

"I drifted, I suppose. I was always hoping that I might find something real." She gave me one of her delicious smiles. "Now I have."

I made the impossible remark. "Could you not have taken a job? Some work you liked?"

"I wasn't trained to work." It was a simple statement. "And I had enough money to live."

50

Of course this was true. Her education had trained her for a suitable marriage and nothing more. Doubtless all her fellow pupils at that French convent were now domestically established, with one or two exceptions who took the veil.

"I wanted to see life, to travel, to find out about myself."

Which I suppose is our common aim, except that you and I, Francis, add that we want to work. Anne's convent did not inspire their young ladies to seek careers.

"I wanted to be happy," she added.

★

I telephoned my agent to complain that I had not received the promised letter from my editor.

"He said he'd write," I wailed.

"He did – to me." My agent expressed no surprise.

"To you?"

"He has reservations. He's thinking about it."

"How long is he going to take? I wouldn't want him to wear out his brain-cells. I hope you were firm."

"About what?" my agent sounded genuinely puzzled. "I think you should consider what he says."

"But, he hasn't bloody well said anything yet! A little encouragement wouldn't come amiss. Does he think I have nerves of steel?"

"He has."

I did not care for my agent's sense of humour. "I suppose he'd like me to write a different kind of book?"

"Probably. Think about it. I'll call you when I hear something more."

Really! It could be said that between them, my agent and publisher were driving me into Anne's arms.

★

Anne enjoyed being taken out to dinner, to the theatre, and it flattered my vanity to notice the way she attracted interest. She had a great sense of style in dress – that simple designer's chic so much talked about – and she moved with a quiet indolence. In public places I was very conscious of her rare physical quality, which is difficult to define precisely, subdued yet sharp though it was. In public places, more than anyone I have ever known, she managed to make the passion in her part of the occasion, with a subtlety of small gestures, lightning flashes of sensuality exchanged. A hand placed casually on one's own, a brush of her lips, a slight body contact, all combined to strengthen my view of the consummate courtesan in her, not forgetting those stealthy glances from her hooded eyes. "You are terribly conventional, Cass," she would say when I ignored these public displays.

I came across old Jawbones in the local café, where we freelances wasted out time drinking coffee.

"Aren't you working?" I said.

"I've had rather a shock." She did look a bit stunned. "I've put up six biographical ideas to my agent. He hasn't sold one of them yet."

"Related ideas? Period-wise, I mean?"

"Oh no! All quite different subjects. Artistic, literary, theatrical and one political."

"You have a preference among the six?"

"It doesn't matter what they choose. I can write on anybody, you know. Can't you?"

"Not easily. Not at all in fact. I'm rather dim. I have to write about someone or something I care about."

"I have to have a commission. It's what publishers respect. They like one to have a definition in mind. I don't think I have the right agent. I must change again."

"I'm inclined to have doubts about mine."

"Of course, you write fiction. That's easy!" She peered confidentially at me. "I saw you the other night at the theatre with rather a smart woman. A new friend?"

"I have lots of new friends. I acquire more each day."
I decided to upset her expectations. "I've a beautiful new
young man. You'd adore him. He's French."

"Um!" She sniffed. "I'm not that keen on foreigners.
I must say, I prefer an English gentleman. Forgive me,
Cass, but aren't you burning the candle at both
ends?"

"Do I look the worse for wear then?"

"Well, no." Her voice held some regret. "I must admit
you look rather well."

I thought of Anne, and mentally sent her a loving
message.

★

Sophia was still raving about her. "She's very witty in that
quiet way of hers," she said. "But my, can she put a man
down – with a look." Then endearingly: "She reminds me
of what I was like when her age."

"I didn't realise you'd had such an interesting life,
Sophia dear," I said, thereby nearly trapping myself into
an admission of knowing more about Anne than Sophia
assumed. I need not have worried.

"Well, of course, I didn't have Anne's advantages.
I wasn't educated abroad. I had to struggle for my
livelihood. Work my fingers to the bone. What it is to be
born rich!"

"I don't think Anne is rich," I said.

"No, perhaps not, but she's lived in the lap of luxury.
That I do know from what she's told me."

I wondered how Anne had related her past to Sophia.
I encouraged further confidences.

"Take that first husband, an Italian Count, a splendid
residence." Sophia sighed. "Some girls are lucky."

I was about to disagree but thought better of it. If Anne
wished to spin fairy tales to Sophia, who was I to break the
spell?

53

Sophia mentioned a man we both knew. "I got him along to meet her. He's in the Foreign Office. I thought that with her languages she would be his cup of tea."

"And wasn't she?"

"They hardly spoke," Sophia admitted defeat. "But then he's probably queer. They all are in the Foreign Office."

"Why don't you find her an older man? The paternal touch, you know." I could never resist teasing Sophia.

"Well, my dear, if they're not married at that age, they're very suspect, you know."

"I hear you've been telling Sophia a lot of Arabian Nights tales," I said to Anne.

She laughed. "Oh, Sophia is easy to deceive. I can't resist it. She wants me to create fantasies about myself. It pleases her." She laughed again. "The trouble is I can't always remember what I do tell her. Not that it matters. She laps it all up."

"Ah! So! And do I lap it all up?"

"You never believe a word I say." She touched my hair.

"Best if I don't, isn't it? It makes for less bones broken."

"Come nearer and I'll tell you something that's absolutely true," she said as she pulled me to her.

It was, I suppose, a new experience for me, in the sense that usually my attachments, my love affairs if you will, were with people generally part of the flow of my life, work and friendships. Anne was a migrant in my life who, for all I knew, at the turn of the equinox, would fly away to another continent. I think it was this quality of impermanence which she carried about her that fascinated me, which created a lingering doubt, a doubt about the truth of everything she said, which excited me as much as did her passionate responses and affirmations. It was possible – yes even at that stage I held this credible – that all her previous encounters in love had been of the same depth of expression, that is with the exception of Maurice, an exception I could easily make, since he was not an enraptured lover of women, merely a man planning escape through marriage. I shall never really know, although one's natural vanity tempts one not to disbelieve. The fact that I found myself questioning everything she said about her past, and indeed about the hours she passed away from me, suggests there was reason to doubt, although I must admit that mine is a temperament which must ever worry a fact given me by a lover. Her "Have you been so much lied to?" came back to me when these doubts crossed my mind. The fault here may have been mine. She was aware of it, even when I did not express it.

"Why do you always question everything I say? Don't pretend you don't. I can feel it, even when you don't speak."

"Well, you fib to Sophia." I evaded her question.

"Sophia enjoys my fibs. I make them specially luscious for her pleasure. Sophia wants to marry me off. Oh well, admittedly, she has great plans for me." She smiled wickedly. "I encourage her imagination."

"But why should I, knowing really so little about you, believe a word you say?" I brought it out.

"Because I am here with you." Her eyes held mine. "That should be proof enough, if you were kind enough."

And there was truth enough in that for me inwardly to flinch at the poverty of my imagination. I might be mean in my acceptance of all she gave, but mean she never was. Even if all her stories were exaggerated, at least they showed she could handle them with a flair that denoted a capacity for life. She had, as it were, expectations from life. That she had suffered disappointments did not lessen her anticipation. As she later told me she was more straightforward than I was. She could make me feel that I was the devious one with my mental cross-examinations.

★

Then the obvious incident occurred. That obvious, yet inevitable, event which lovers always come up against, and which, so often, creates a first tension in trust.

It was an evening when she had pressed me to cancel an appointment with an American editor.

"But I can't," I said. "He wants me to do some work for him. That means dollars, darling. I might be able to take you to Venice."

"Couldn't you make another date? I don't want to be at home tonight."

All this was on the telephone. "Why not?" I asked.

"Well, someone might arrive whom I don't want to see."

"Well, don't." Then I asked. "Someone from your past?"

"In a way, in a way. Naturally you can't cancel. I'll stay at home and think of you."

My American and I were to dine at the Connaught, where he was staying. Soon, he was telling me what a bitch his ex-wife was. In order to show an amiable disposition, I invented an ex-husband. I described your characteristics, Francis, to him. He was moved to pity for me. "That's some chauvinist pig!" he said. We had a few drinks in the bar and, rather later than expected, went into the grill-room. As you know I am awfully short-sighted, so at first I did not see Anne and her escort, a few tables away. The man seemed ordinary, thinnish, darkish hair, with rather pinched features. Anne was wearing her dark glasses, a habit she had when low in spirits. So much, I told myself, of an evening at home thinking about me. I began to flirt with my American. Then she saw me. I gave her a breezy wave. I do not know at what stage of their meal they were at, but shortly after that Anne rose, quickly. The man tried hurriedly to attract the waiter's attention. Anne walked towards the foyer, pausing, fractionally, at our table, touched me lightly on the hand, and murmured, "I'll phone you." The man was still trying to get the waiter to hurry up with the bill.

"Quite a glamour-puss!" My American looked at Anne retreating.

I got home late. The phone was ringing. I let it ring.

It started up again.

56

I took the words out of her mouth. "Not interested. Don't want to know. Entirely your business."

"Will you please listen to me?" She sounded angry.

The man, whose name she told me and which I instantly forgot, was the person she had not wished to be at home to. He and his wife, so she said, rented a villa next to the one she and Maurice had in Spain, and both witnessed Maurice's turbulent and violent behaviour.

"He was very kind," she said. "No, I did not sleep with him. He is married, I tell you."

"Poo!" I said. "Why should that stop you? He appeared quite fond this evening."

"He harasses me. Yes, I admit, he just wants the usual. But I've always turned him down. And ever would. He still persists. He's helpful in some ways. He takes me and the child out for drives. The parents like him. Maurice hates him because he hit Maurice once when he threatened me."

"You've had a fascinating life," I said nastily, totting up her admission that in the daytime she saw other people. Other people that is apart from family, and Sophia.

"I'm getting in a taxi now and I'm coming."

"I'm pissed," I said.

"I don't mind." She cut off.

Sure enough she came, and through my tiredness induced by too much drink with my American, I heard more about this man, his wife, and their involvement in her matrimonial troubles. I did not quite believe her denial of him as one of her lovers, yet it was possible. She did not deny that he wanted to be, and that he was obviously obsessed by her. That I did believe. She only saw him, she said, on the strict understanding that he kept his place.

"And if you think I can't control a man, you're very wrong, my darling. I take what I want and that's that."

A hardness in her tone made me revert to the courtesan image I had invented for her.

It was the only time I saw this man, yet I saw him distinctly enough to be able to place him when his appearance was later described to me. I did in fact believe

57

her when she said she had always kept him at bay. Somehow he did not fit into the general portrait I had gained of her previous lovers. They had all been young men, and this man was in his late forties, at least. They had been lively, high-spirited, fun-loving. He gave an impression of a man suppressed, emotionally. A conservative man, inhibited, domesticated, with no spark to him. Then clearly what Anne had very definitely required in her lovers was youth and a bright jazzy personality, and, rather important this, some culture, which Maurice had. Roberto painted and had pretensions in that field. Craig wrote plays no one produced, and Erik, the Finn, was a dedicated musician. This man looked, one might say, beneath her, yet there was something sinister about his inexorable attentiveness which suggested that he was biding his time, waiting for the opportunity. The opportunity when it came, as I will tell you, rebounded on him with disastrous consequences. I thought all this, more or less, not perhaps so clearly, as I half dozed on her body.

"He has the look of a man who would get his own way. A man who does his sums correctly," I summed up my thoughts about him.

"Not with me. I've dealt with many of his kind in my time."

"I'm not jealous," I muttered.

"I am, darling, jealous of everyone you've ever loved before me. Jealous of everyone you'll love after me."

"You visualise the possibility of the future?" I was less tired.

"I hate the future. I can't see the future. I won't see the future." She was vehement. "I've never had a future."

It was so appallingly sad at that moment that I did not know how to erase what had been such years of unhappiness, or at least years of void. She had chosen to select me as some symbol of possible happiness, and I was dreadfully conscious of how easily I could, would probably, smash that illusion.

I was, you see, beginning to feel responsible for her, which, in an affair, is a point when one gets up and goes, for fear of piling up the ultimate grief, or stops, as I then resolved I would, which in a way is the action of a coward. Therefore in the morning when I found her gone, I sat down and wrote her another, a third letter of love, brief yet sincere, more genuine than the previous two. These were, dear Francis, the letters found under her pillow.

★

I decided that we should have a whole day out together. When I telephoned her the next morning, she mentioned the child.

"Well," I said, "surely your parents can look after her for one day?"

"Perhaps my sister will," she said.

This knocked me back. She had never mentioned a sister. For all I knew there might be brothers, cousins, a whole circle of relatives. She should have been christened Calypso, "she who conceals".

"She's a very selfish hippy, but I'll make it worth her while."

The month was September, and the day as deliciously crisp and sun-filled as only a September day at its best can be. I thought we would drive into the country. I planned to break my strange resolution about not introducing her to any of my friends, and drop in on my darling Rick, who, with his gentleness and quietude of spirit, would be kind to her. I told her about him as we drove through leafy lanes glistening with autumnal colours. Told her about Rick's work, his sculpture, his dedication, his loving charity to all, and the beneficial role he played in my life.

"Unlike you, darling" – I spoke gaily – "I don't go to church when I'm confused. I go to Rick."

"Have you told him about me?" she asked, then added: "I haven't been to church for a long time now."

Later I found this was untrue, that during all the time of our association she had been seeing a Jesuit father.

"He doesn't know we're coming. Rick never asks questions. He feels no need of them. He accepts what he sees."

"Shall I pass the test?"

I glanced at her, at my side. She transmitted a feeling of joy of the kind I had never yet felt in her. She was relaxed, shorn of the edge of strain which always was part of her, except in love. I realised what it was that struck me, and indeed others, about her image of sophistication, what in fact arrested attention. An element of injury suffered, a stigma, invisible to the naked eye, yet sentient, attracting brutal responses as some wounded animals attract attack from their kind – indeed as do human beings, more so perhaps. She was, I knew at that moment, wholly defence-less. Fancifully one might have said that she was innocence unprotected, an object of beauty which excited the violator. Perhaps this is what Father Luke meant when he described her as vulnerable.

That day she was trusting me, and that day was good. She had given me her love and passion, yet never before her trust, simply because trust in relation to others was no part of her past experience. Father Luke, had he caught her early, might have advised a closed order for her, which would have been an easy way out, with its discipline and prayer and gravity. Circumstances however had thrust her into the worldly life and, trained by her conventual education to respond, she had done so. I mention this, which is not such a flight of fancy as it would seem, because she was a Catholic, and because her faith was to be an important consideration in the final stages of this story.

"I've got a present for you."

She brought it from her handbag, as we sat in a wood-land dell over our picnic lunch. A copy of Sir Thomas Wyatt's poems. That line, *Was I ever yet of your love grieved*, still haunts me with the memory of that day. She often wished to give me things, and this I stopped, after the first gift of a pair of mother-of-pearl cuff-links. What did I give her, you may ask? Oh, the conventional tokens exchanged between lovers – flowers, scent, records.

She then told me, almost in an offhand tone, that she had an unfinished manuscript she had written about Wyatt and Anne Boleyn. She had become interested in the subject while at the retreat, part of which, the original castle (now the residential area for guests), was in fact Wyatt's birthplace. Anne had used the library for her research. One of the long galleries at the retreat is rumoured to have been Henry VIII's spy-glass where, through its long windows, he verified his accusations against Anne Boleyn as she flirted with Wyatt, with Sir Henry Norris and others.

"Henry," said Anne, "swore that Anne Boleyn committed adultery with a hundred men." She gave me a sly look. "In actual fact no adultery was ever really proved against her."

"I never appreciated you were so learned," I said.

As I spoke I could understand why Anne was attracted to Anne Boleyn's history, she whom gossip and slander convicted of unbounded libidinosity, whereas, as later more precise historians proved, all that could in fact be levelled at this Tudor Anne was flirtatiousness, high spirits, and an addiction to dancing, poetry and music. Only one convicted lover had confessed to sexual intimacy, Mark Smeaton, and that under torture by Thomas Cromwell.

I was fascinated by Anne's interest having carried itself to actual manuscript stage. Why had she not finished it, I asked.

"I married Maurice." A simple statement of fact. "I'll show you what I've written – sometime."

I never did see that unfinished enquiry into Wyatt's passion for Anne Boleyn. I wonder what has happened to that manuscript. She had never, until then, mentioned any personal interest in writing, although she was always questioning me about my work. Was this modesty or secrecy?

She told me more about her convent schooling, which, evidently, she had much enjoyed. An expensive French establishment, staffed (if that is the word) by extremely well educated nuns. Manners and deportment featured high on the curriculum. Anne's godmother paid the fees. This was followed by a period in Florence, at one of those semi-tutorial establishments, where young ladies were introduced to the appreciation of the arts. It was there that Anne met Roberto, when she was nineteen, or rather where Roberto met her and persuaded her to live with him.

"What I liked about the convent," she said, "was that every hour was arranged for one. Agreeably so. Those were my happy years. No worries, no threats, no doubts."

This kind of education accounted for the cosmopolitan flavour of her sophistication, and one that attracted me, being familiar to me, since I have, as you know, a foreign upbringing, although mine should be described as pagan, certainly not Catholic. Anne planned to have her child similarly educated. Through you, Francis, the child, your ward, has received a foreign education, in Protestant Switzerland however, which from what you tell me ("A charming, intelligent, yet basically boring young woman") has saved her from Anne's Jesuitical heritage.

"I've no doubts now," she said, "about you." She laughed. "You're the doubting Thomas."

Because the day was fair I made a denial, which, in fact, was sincere. That day it was possible to fantasise about permanence, while simultaneously appreciating that practical difficulties (the child for instance) made the idea ludicrously impossible. Beware of bright September days which mock all reason and logic and entertain, not unawares, glimpses of a preposterous paradise. Thinking back to that day now, I am conscious of caution in this attempt to convey the wholly new sense of ease which came from Anne. Possibly landscape of trees and country in their autumnal magnificence to the eye spread a tenderness and harmony which was lacking in her life, and, as it were, simplified her reactions that day. Equally our picnic might have reminded her of festivities enjoyed with the nuns (*fêtes de campagne* outings) and her fellow pupils at a time when there was no menace in her life.

Then again – and here speaks the doubting Thomas in me – she may have been wanting to appear as some carefree natural creature in keeping with this day out in the country with me.

We arrived at Rick's, bearing honey and scones bought at a village shop. You know that endearing way Rick has of greeting a stranger with a long loving scrutiny. His gentleness was even more evident as he took charge of Anne, showing her his domain – his studio and garden. He made us tea, and treated Anne as though he had known her as long as he had known me. Again I was aware of the possibility of a future with Anne, the possibility of her fitting in with my friends, which sounds presumptuous, yet indicated that I was considering that future, which until then had been dismissed. Rick made Anne laugh, recounting several silly times he and I had known together.

"I've known Cass almost all my life," Rick told Anne. "We first met at a Swiss lakeside Kursaal when I was a frightfully precocious adolescent. Our respective families were taking tea, as they said, to the background of light music. We walked in the Kursaal gardens and spoke about life, in capital letters. Cass was dressed in a white sailor suit, very fetching. We made a couple of smart adolescents – or so we thought."

Anne pressed him for further memories and, between Rick and myself, we brought out our shared joys of years of friendship.

"I envy Rick," she said later. "He's known so much of you."

Altogether the calling on Rick was a success, matching the balm of that September day. When Rick took Anne's hands in his, a habit he has in his farewells, he said in that soft voice of his:

"You mustn't be sad. You're not made for sadness."

The sound and sense of Rick's farewell to Anne remains in my mind, because it was so tragically true. She was indeed not made for sadness, simply because she had sought so desperately for happiness as an inner faith of

63

what was due to her. That at this time she equated happiness with me was evident in her obsessive affirmation of it when we were together. That day I felt that in no way could I undermine by doubt her bright conviction.

Over dinner, which we had at some riverside hotel, she told me that she had received, that morning, a letter from a friend of Maurice, telling her that Maurice was a very sick man and could not be expected to live many years if he continued drinking and behaving as he did. The letter then went on to plead Maurice's cause, to restate his love for the child, and – to Anne, the most fearful item – to declare that Maurice was prepared to become a member of her Church if she would consent to take him back. It was sheer blackmail. She told me all this quietly, without any of her usual panic. I was the one to express disgust and anger.

"I'm not going to be blackmailed through my religion," she said. "You've wondered, haven't you, why I haven't done anything about getting a place of my own. It's been the thought of Maurice banging on my front-door which stops me. At least, at the parents', I'm moderately protected. Yet I know I must make a decision."

I looked at her fearfully. She was smiling at me. The quiet day had somehow enhanced her.

"Whatever happens, I want you to know that everything I've ever said to you, everything I've ever been, is absolutely true, for ever. Nothing in the future can or will alter that. You've given me a lot."

"I haven't given you so much." I faced my inadequacies where she was concerned.

"The beginning of us was strange, and so on and so on. I've never been so forward. I astonished myself. For me it was unexpected. For you perhaps not. It would take too much time to explain fully, and we don't have that much time. I've never given myself before. I embarrass you when I say that." She laughed at me. "You've a prudish streak in you, Cass dear. I don't expect you to feel the same as I do. In some ways, Cass, you are less straightforward than I am."

There was possibly a truth here. I wondered why she had slipped in the remark about not having much time. It was almost as though she were unconscious of her use of it.

"Are you trying to tell me that you might take Maurice back?" I asked.

"No, not that. That never. The pressures on me, Cass, are very great. I must, I have to, sort it all out." She placed her hand on mine. "It's been a beautiful day, Cass, a beautiful day."

We drove back more or less in silence. She fell asleep almost immediately. I let her sleep through until the morning. She refused breakfast, and, at parting, held me tightly, looking into my face with a steadiness which disconcerted me. Was she, I ask myself now, memorising my features for a future which did not contain us?

"I'll come to you soon, soon," she said. Then added what at the time I disregarded as an irrelevancy: "Trust me."

What had she to sort out with Maurice? I asked myself. I did not then know what Sophia was to tell me so dramatically, so shortly after this.

Thinking back, I wonder now, whether I had any presentiment of the tragedy that followed. I could not quite understand why suddenly I should feel so haunted by those eyes. I do not think it fallacious to say that my involvement, which had now reached a deeper degree, gave me an intensity of unease which proved not to be false. I might be carrying this fancy further when I say that possibly what I felt at our first meeting – a mixture of disquiet and irritation – may have been an instinctual premonition of undefined disaster related to Anne. Some people carry about them an aspect of danger to others and to themselves. How had Rick, knowing nothing of her except her presence, put his finger on the sadness in Anne – particularly intuitive this – on a day when she was relaxed and at ease.

I rationalised all this by telling myself that our last meeting had not been on the level of previous encounters.

For one thing there was no expression of sexual love, merely a knowledge that it was there.

"We don't have to confirm it every time," she had said. "If we were miles apart, months, years apart, my love, it would always be there – for me."

She had, in some way that day, presented an unknown facet of herself with her ease of manner, shown me a more self-contained affirmative personality. She had been less the courtesan in my fantasy of her than a person with problems which she had resolved to solve. I had been taken into account as a positive quantity in her life, my responsibility in this discounted. Her excursion into creativity, the Wyatt-Anne Boleyn investigation, showed that she was capable of independent action, although she had not finished it when marriage to Maurice re-arranged her life. It did cross my mind, so habit-forming was my questioning everything she said, initially as a joke, that this may have been sheer invention on her part. She had not, as most authors do, offered any detail about her research, line of enquiry or potential conclusions. I was genuinely confused. Had I created for my amused pleasure an untrue portrait?

*

My agent telephoned.

"He'll publish if you agree to certain cuts."

"Cuts? I thought he was buggering on about more length. What cuts?"

"Easy to make. I said you'd do it."

"Suppose I won't?"

He ignored that. "Of course, there won't be much money in it. You can't expect it."

"How much?" I thought of Sophia's "pittance".

"Don't know yet. You'd better get started on another."

"When's he going to see me?"

"He's gone to New York."

"I hope his plane crashes into the Atlantic – a slow drowning."

"I think he's been most fair. Not easy, Cass, to get a publisher to say anything these days."

"Who the hell said it was ever easy?"

"I'll write and confirm you agree." He put down the phone before I could give vent to my fury.

I recalled Ivy Compton-Burnett describing a writer's life as "that extra occupation". There was nothing left for me to do except think about Anne.

Everything I have described to you about Anne is true, although how truly do we describe a lover? Indeed how much do we, can we know? You once said, dear Francis, that one knows more about a stranger in love than about an intimate. Possibly there is truth in that since the stranger does not bother with concealment, and since what we gain in insight in such instances is not matter to be added up, subtracted from, assessed and re-assessed as one invariably does in a longer relationship. The knowing of a lover inevitably engenders agony because the longer the chosen one is part of one's daily life, the longer the channels of introspective enquiry. The continuation of love is a continuation of agony, of joy too, admittedly, and now that I have reached a stage in my life when I am no longer afflicted with having to examine and re-examine every word and gesture of a loved one, I consider myself as one finally fortunate, being in possession only of myself, and yet what a lack I sense in my life.

What, I wondered, had attracted Maurice to her? Considering that he was not a man usually attracted to women. She had clearly been compassionate to his shattered life and despair. Did Maurice for a while suppose that he could offer her the attentiveness of a stable relationship? Or did something in her tell him that sexually she would not require too much from him? "He married me," she once said, "so that he could hate me." Why had she consented? Because she was, temperamentally, incapable of disagreeing with another person's decision about herself? Perhaps it was all very simple: they both felt that they could settle

67

down peacefully and friendlily with each other, mutual comfort being the aim since both needed comfort from recent personal disasters. I thought a lot about this after that day in the country with Anne. Short though their marriage had been, they had lived together for four of its five years, time enough to forge links, however distasteful or limiting these may have been. Thinking about the letter Anne had received from Maurice's friend, I wondered whether he was really ill, or whether all this was another ploy to invoke her pity and charity. Surely, I told myself, she would not go back to him, since that would certainly lead to further unhappiness, yet I had my fears. I was, you will note, not so unconcerned as I had previously prided myself on being.

★

I felt great relief when she telephoned a few days later (she had sent a telegram thanking me for "the beautiful day"), relief that we were still in touch, relief to be shattered when I recognised the old note of panic again in her voice.

"Everything is closing on me," she said, then went on to tell me that Maurice had written to say that he must talk to her about the future. "Their future," he called it. He would, he said, call on her very shortly.

"Why not refuse to see him?" I asked.

This clearly at the moment did not strike her as a possible action.

"He's determined to come. I must get away. I'm going now."

I tried to reason with her, urged her to come and see me. "Come at once, please." For a few seconds I thought she would agree.

"My bag is packed. I must get away. By myself for a few days."

I used every kind of persuasion, even suggesting that we could spend a few days away together.

Her panic increased as we spoke.

"Only a few days, to sort myself out, so that I can face what has to be done."

"Where are you going?"

She mumbled something about getting as far away as possible. Again I pressed her to come to me. Again she appeared to hesitate.

"Darling, I have to get away. Please understand. I promise you I'll be back soon – very soon with you. Just a few days I need, to sort it all out. Trust me."

It crossed my mind that she might be planning to go to the retreat and, thinking this, I stopped insisting.

"I love you," she said as she put the phone down.

★

Appositely, it was Sophia who telephoned to relate an astonishing fact.

"Did you know that Anne isn't divorced from Maurice?"

"Don't be stupid, Sophia, it can't be." I was about to add that Father Luke had spoken to me about the divorce, then realised that in fact he had merely referred to a "separation", which was the word I had used when speaking to him out of deference to his calling.

"Well, I've had it from Maurice himself. Mind you, Anne never actually told me she was divorced." Sophia gave an audible sigh. "I just took it for granted, because you told me, Cass."

What could I say? Deflated hardly expressed my reaction to this news. A few minutes later I picked up the phone in a rage. Perhaps she had even lied to me about going away. I recognised the mother's voice, as she told me that Anne was not there. When would she be back I enquired?

"I don't quite know. She's touring."

I could have screamed. Anne had no car and did not drive. Why lie to me about the divorce? I looked at her second letter again. Yes, it was reasonably clear. *Maurice and I are divorced. I'm R.C. so it's all been pretty ghastly.* Then – something which I would not have done some weeks before – I gave her a let-out, speculating that perhaps, just perhaps, the word "being" had been left out before "divorced". She always wrote a hasty hand, I reminded myself. The pressures, the great pressures, she felt burdened by explained themselves now. As a Catholic, divorce was not a light decision for her to take. All her education had stressed that. "It's all been pretty ghastly," when related to her faith, became clear.

You can imagine, Francis, how I felt. Angry, exasperated, confused, frustrated because I could not even reach her to confront her with these inconsistencies. Had I been deceived? And yet what had I been deceived about? A freakish element pervaded my reaction. I had not entered into an enduring relationship. I had always told myself that Anne was peripheral to my life, or had I? I had kept up a running pretence of not believing a word she said. Then why did I feel so outraged? The matter of the divorce was a misunderstanding I could settle to my own satisfaction. Anne herself, I must admit, never mentioned the word divorce to me. When I invited Sophia and Guy to that first dinner with Anne, I mentioned she was divorced from Maurice, knowing this would attract Sophia's curiosity. I allowed myself a grin at the thought of the collapse of Sophia's match-making schemes.

With whom was Anne touring? Hardly Maurice, since his licence had long been suspended for drunken driving. Her bag was packed, she had said when she had spoken to me. Was the driver of the car there standing at her side? Why had she not told me this? After all, I was apt to say to her that all her actions were no concern of mine – that is, her actions away from me. I could hardly ring the parents and ask. For all I knew, she might have a brother. She had, as it were, suddenly produced a sister out of the hat.

I can see you mocking slightly, dear Francis – friendly mockery, I trust – at the emotional situation I found myself in, going round and round the mulberry bush of pros and cons, of motive, of intention. Through my exasperation I realised that my involvement had changed, had probably been in the process of change for some time,

70

from one uncommitted to one personally anxious. I waited for the usual letter. None came through the post, and no telephone call.

Four days later, with still no news, I phoned the parents again, enquiring, in as bland a tone as I could muster, whether they had any idea when Anne would be back. The phone was slammed down on me. I was frantic, my imagination soared with bleak possibilities. I was left with no other recourse but to go to Sophia. I went round to her house. I admitted my concern and my involvement.

At first Sophia contented herself with quite a mild comment – "Well really, Cass, you did take me in" – and then phoned the parental number. "They're not answering," she said.

I was not, however, to escape Sophia's further comments.

"Mind you," she almost sniffed, "I always thought there was something odd about Anne. All those men I invited especially for her. Never a response. Something very deep there. I sensed it."

"You think she's perfect. Frankness personified."

She ignored that. "These very sexy-looking women are always dubious – fishy. One thing about her strikes me. She's never mentioned you to me. Deceitful that! I suppose she wants a change though. A woman used to men, it's to be expected. Really, Cass, you do get yourself into messes. Of course, she is foreign."

"Foreign?" I could not follow Sophia's reasoning.

"All that Continental upbringing. Like you. It makes one think."

"Oh, I assure you, Sophia, the English are not immune to such tastes." I made it snappish.

"I can see she's attractive. I should have known you couldn't resist. I did say to Guy, if I were that way inclined – which I'm not – Anne would attract me. She's probably gone off for good, you know. Had enough. You're very demanding, Cass."

I wanted to laugh, but could not, because I sensed that Anne's disappearance had less simple an explanation.

"Bill once accused me of having an affair with that

Greek poet girl. Men are always jealous of friendship between women. And, if the truth be told, get a kick out of thinking about them in bed. I said to Bill: 'What about your schoolboy involvement with your mates?' That, of course, is just good fellowship. Women are suspect. Women are always suspect, unless they're worshipping the male." She paused for breath. "Men say women have a penis envy. I say men have a penis self-love. It's not all that marvellous at times! Tell a man that, and you've made an enemy for life. I can't understand why, Cass, knowing you've got to settle down and think about your future, you embarked on this. You're irresponsible, Cass. You've no time for love affairs at the moment." Then suddenly gentle, "Is she very lovely? In bed?"

"Fabulous, wouldn't you say, Sophia?" I spoke lightly. "Mysterious, sensual, erotic – you name it. Actually, a spoilt child. You once said I was."

"Oh!" Sophia gave one of her deepest sighs. "I do know what it's like to be in love. Wonderful, and debilitating. Sheer hell really!"

"I'm not in love with Anne. Something less, yet just as habit-forming."

"You'd better end it anyway. It can lead to no good. I'll find out where she is. Don't worry, Cass. I do wish you were settled again."

"Thank you, Sophia. I'd like to know she's all right. That's all," I said, as I left.

★

Later that night Sophia called on me. I could see from her whole manner that her news was not pleasant.

"She's dead," she said. "Suicide. An overdose."

I could not believe it, and hardly took in the few details Sophia gave. Some roadside hotel outside a small market town. The police were dealing with the case. It was complicated.

"Three of your letters, Cass, were found under her pillow." Sophia was unusually gentle. "And a letter written to you in her handbag."

"She couldn't commit suicide. She's a Catholic – it's a mortal sin," was all that I could say.

"Well she took enough tablets to kill two people." Where Sophia got her information from I did not bother to ask. "An inquest is being held."

"If it's suicide she won't be buried in consecrated ground. It can't be, it mustn't be."

"What does it matter how she's buried?" Sophia said.

"It matters to her." I was insistent. "She is – was – a Catholic. I'll phone the police."

"Sleep on it," Sophia urged.

Today, doubtless, Catholics are less troubled about divorce and suicide, at least this is the general assumption, although, in my experience of them, even today, their liberal views, when put to the test, usually revert, at a moment of personal judgement, to the strictures of their religious teaching.

I was already busy on the telephone. Sophia, practical in emergencies, placed a whisky near my hand. I gulped it down. Then I got through to the small market town where Anne had died. I gave my name and mentioned Anne by her married title. The man at the other end said he would fetch the Inspector or Detective-Sergeant, I can't remember which, dealing with the case. His name was Thame. He was quiet, helpful. My name was familiar to him. I blurted out my information that Anne was a Catholic, that surely it must have been an accident, that she suffered from insomnia, that I knew she had every intention of returning to London.

"Yes," Thame said. "The letter found in her handbag, addressed to you, gives a date for her return. But I rather think it was deliberate."

"Please," I begged. "You must understand her religion was important to her. Suicide would have" – I hesitated – "affronted her."

"I will weigh all the evidence," he said.

"Do you want me to come to the inquest?" I asked.

"I don't think that will be necessary. You could come the day after. I'll let you know when the inquest is to take place."

"I will," I said. "I'll ring you when I get there."

"Thank you for calling," he said. He sounded as though he meant it.

I kept him a minute longer, driven to the question. "Her companion?" The query was in my voice.

His tone was dry. "We've tracked him down."

"Was all that wise?" Sophia asked, and what was so extraordinary, in view of Sophia's relish for detail, she never asked me anything else. All she said was, "I'm very sorry, Cass."

★

In the morning I phoned Father Luke at the retreat. He did not interrupt as I told him the whole tragic story, hiding nothing about my relationship with Anne.

"I'm terribly sorry," he said. "I hope it wasn't suicide. If it was, it certainly would have been under intolerable stress, with the minimum of culpability. I'll phone the parish priest at the town you mention and do what I can about the burial." He paused. "There are limits to what human beings can stand. I should think Anne had been very near that limit."

"I wonder who the companion was?" I had to say it.

"Rumours of some association have been circulating hereabouts for a good while. I always thought it was a fiction on Maurice's part. I still do. If it had anything in it Anne would have told you."

His was a better faith than mine, and I silently blessed his generosity.

"You mustn't go the inquest," he added. "Salt on the wound is indulgence. Go later, in peace. I will pray for you." Then, as though there were a link. "I will say some Masses for Anne."

I do not, as you know, Francis, hold any religious faith, but I pray in my fashion that I will always respond to another's distress as did Father Luke with his restoring touch.

When the chips are down the best, or the worst, comes out, and I was glad that Sophia finally fitted into the former category. There was much about Sophia that was infuriating, yet basically there was a kindness, admittedly often concealed in her dotty malice, and an honesty expressed mostly to disturb her friends. Knowing her for such a long time – as we both did – one grew to appreciate the virtues which she so recklessly hid from casual acquaintances. I had expected her to dash into some barbed observations, almost anticipated her telling me that she had always considered Anne to be neurotic, and that her suicide was an inevitable character-flaw. The fact that, at a moment of tragedy, Sophia should have shown restraint, was a gentle reminder that she really cared not only about our friendship, but about other people.

★

I drove to the market town on the day following the inquest. One of those inconspicuous places, with a couple of hotels. I must have arrived on early-closing day, because all the shops were shut, and there were few people about in the streets. It was still that beautiful September weather, yet in that late afternoon there was a chill in the air. I parked the car, and walked into what looked the most possible hotel and booked a room. "Dinner at seven-thirty," the receptionist told me in a bored voice. My room overlooked the market square. I picked up the phone and asked to be connected with the police station. I could not remember what rank Thame held. I garbled Inspector-detective-sergeant together as one word.

"You want the Coroner's office." A voice gave me the number.

I got through.

"Hello," Thame said, in quite a chatty way.

"When would you like to see me?" I asked.

"Any time. Where are you staying? Yes, I know it. I'll be along about six-thirty."

I thought it rather considerate of him to come to me. After a wash and brush-up, I went downstairs to the lounge. There were few other guests. I could see the entrance from where I sat, and recognised Thame as he walked in through the door, because he did not potter about as did the residents. He was a tall man, dark-haired, with a pleasant open face, somewhere in his early forties I judged. He was in plain clothes. Through the banalities of introduction and the ordering of drinks, I knew he was mildly scrutinising me, summing me up, I suppose, in a sort of trained fashion.

"It's been a shock for you. I'm very sorry." He sounded kind. "I'm glad you didn't come to the inquest," he said. "It was unpleasant."

He might have been younger than I had first assumed. His was the kind of face which does not alter much over the years.

"I daresay any inquest is unpleasant," I said.

"Not always. This one wasn't nice at all." A tinge of condemnation in his tone. "You'll want me to tell you all about it." Statement from him rather than query.

"Please."

"It was the people. They weren't nice people at all. Though I felt sorry, rather, for the husband. He seemed a decent enough chap in his way. A gentleman."

So always did Maurice strike other men, I cynically thought.

"Everything, please, I want to hear everything," I stressed.

"Do you know" – he smiled at me – "you were the only one to come forward?"

I felt, metaphorically, patted on the head.

"Could you, do you mind, begin at the beginning?" I asked.

"Which beginning?" He was brighter than I had reckoned. "You mean when we came on the scene at the hotel?" Then almost irrelevantly. "She was a beautiful young woman. Yes, beautiful. Of course," he surprisingly added, "I only saw her naked."

His image, starkly put, gave me the picture.

"A shifty character, the man." He paused. "Do you know him?"

I nodded negatively. Then asked quickly. "What does he look like?"

"Thinnish sort of chap, early fifties, darkish, peakish, shifty." He came back to that. "A businessman of sorts."

He had placed him for me. I knew now it was the man who had dined Anne at the Connaught. The one who, I had anticipated, "would do his sums correctly".

"Quiet voice, sly I'd say. A liar we proved. Jittery. His wife was in court, watching him all the time." Thame appeared to relish the thought. "You know he did a bunk, don't you?"

"I know nothing," I said.

"Yes, when the hotel people were waiting for the doctor to arrive. He bunked – bunked. Drove off in his car." Thame watched my expression. "Ah! Not nice was it, not nice at all. We didn't have much trouble finding him. The hotel proprietor's wife, Mrs. Stanley, took the precaution of noting down his car number. She's that kind. I reckon she does that automatically."

"Look, why don't you have dinner with me?" I appreciated that it would take Thame some time to cover all he had to tell. "That's if you're free."

He accepted. "Yes, you'll want to know everything, won't you?" He gave me a shrewd look. His eyes were brown, the sort of boyish brown of men who retain their youth better than most. "That's what you've come for, isn't it? To know everything."

Over dinner, probably because the tables were close to each other in that small room, he talked generalities, although these were chosen to enable him to place me, socially and professionally. So I gave him, as briefly as possible, what he would consider relevant personal information.

"I couldn't live in London," he said. "I come from Shropshire." This accounted for his slight country accent. "Moved to these parts when I married."

This required interest from me, and I elicited that he had two adolescent daughters.

"I'd have liked a boy," he said. "But the wife doesn't want any more. She's the practical one."

There was something in the way he said this that made me wonder about him.

"There's a child, isn't there?" He was back to Anne.

As we drifted into the lounge for coffee and drinks, I said: "Let's get back to that scene at the hotel, shall we?"

A desolate, sordid little tale Thame told. The hotel, a kind of roadhouse, run by a bossy woman and her apathetic husband, with a minimal staff. Anne and the man had been there three days.

"I've written down the name for you. You'll want to go there, won't you?" he said.

How did he know? I asked myself as he handed over a sheet of paper with, I quickly noted, some road directions on it. He continued his story, placing the details before me as though literally extracted from his report. The man leaving before the doctor arrived. The "massive" overdose that no amount of resuscitation techniques could counteract. They had taken her to the local infirmary, where she did not regain consciousness.

"No natural cause of death was found when the pathologist carried out the post-mortem," Thame said. "The verdict recorded was that she had taken a massive dose of pento-barbitone accidentally."

I became alert. "Accidentally you say?"

"Yes. Your telephone statement was taken into account. And the letter addressed to you in her handbag gives a date for her return." Then he explained his position. "I'm the Coroner's officer. I carried out the investigation, interviewed the witnesses, and wrote the final report." He gave me a smile. "She'd been taking a hell of a lot of pills.

I checked with several London chemists. In view of what you told me, and other evidence, my report gave her the benefit of the doubt."

We looked at each other. I knew and he knew that the pathologist's "massive" dose did not quite tally with "accidentally". What had moved him to stretch the verdict?

"I'm speaking to you as a friend," he explained. "I've seen everyone now connected with this case. I haven't liked what I've seen. Except you." It was a simple statement.

"I was very fond of her," I told him.

"Yes, I know, a beautiful friendship."

I looked at him sharply. There was no hint of cynicism or of *double entendre* in his manner. Yet surely, I thought, he had read the letters. He then told me about Maurice, who had had to be summoned back when he was already on his way to Spain. It was clear that, although Thame felt some contempt for him, he forgave him much.

"I believe he's a sick man," he said.

Furthermore, I gathered that Maurice, as a witness, had been discreet, mentioning that their marriage had been happy in the beginning, that Anne had, unfortunately, been addicted to sleeping pills before he had met her.

"He looked surprised when your name was mentioned," Thame said.

"In what way mentioned?"

"Only as the person to whom she wrote her last letter." Thame smiled. "It wasn't necessary to mention your letters in court – those found under her pillow. That was private."

He was surprising me more and more. Why, I wondered, was he so considerate? I tackled him.

"Did you read the letters?"

"Yes." He sounded apologetic. "It was part of my job to do so. We've got them safe. No one claimed them. They're on the shelf."

Then it was that he explained "the shelf" to me – an inter-office classification for the safe-keeping of unclaimed papers.

"No one read them except me," Thame continued. "Mind you, I wouldn't put anything past the man. Though I'd guess she kept them pretty well out of his sight."

I was astonished at his imagination, altogether puzzled by this soft-spoken, tall man who came from Shropshire and whose life was, as far as I knew, so very ordinary.

"They met abroad, the two couples." He told me what I already knew.

"He hung around her when the marriage broke up. He gave his evidence in a slimy way. Contradicted himself several times. Said she was worried because the husband was harassing her. Wanted to get away for a few days. He offered to drive her to Cornwall, and they stopped here on the way. Said she was nervous, ill, undecided, so they booked in at Mrs. Stanley's place. The husband looked at him as though he were something the cat sicked up. My opinion of him is low, very low." He looked at me with some concern. "You're tired. Best get some sleep."

"The cemetery," I asked. "Where is it?"

He gave me the directions. He drew an envelope from his pocket.

"This is a copy of her letter to you. We have to keep the original," he said. "It belongs to you. I'll call tomorrow. You have dinner with me."

I was enormously tired, and flummoxed – there is no better word – by Thame, the Coroner's officer, the man to whom Anne owed her proper Catholic burial. He had become personally involved, which I would have thought contrary to regulations. He had taken against the parents, was full of contempt for the man, and somehow appreciated that Maurice was a damaged character. He had decided to accept me. I felt that if he had not liked me he would not have given me the copy of Anne's last letter to me.

You can imagine, dear Francis, how disturbing it was for me to read that typewritten copy of the letter she never posted. *Darling*, she wrote, *Am leaving for Cornwall. Brute force moves me.* She went on to tell me what she had

80

told me on the telephone, that Maurice was determined to confront her. *I feel absolutely trapped. And* – this heavily underlined – *I'm not running from you! Just running! I need complete seclusion for a while.* Then, as Thame had told me, she gave a date for her return. The last line was almost unbearable to read: *Hello darling and au-revoir. I love you. Anne.*

Oh, there was one other sentence in the letter which struck horror into me, and my first instinct was to forget about it, even keep it from you, Francis. *All my hair is cut short,* she wrote. *I look like a shorn lamb ready for the slaughter.* I was at first appalled that her lovely auburn hair, which she wore at neck length, had been in any way savaged. Then this grisly detail in that prophetic sentence struck me as a premeditated action, getting herself ready for the block as it were. Was Anne Boleyn's hair cut before her execution? It appeared to me, this cutting of hair, to be a psychological admission. It was so unlike any of her gestures. I had often expressed my delight in her wavy auburn crop, shining so immaculately, so well groomed. I would watch her brushing it, reminded, I must admit, of my mother's sensuous movements as she brushed her hair with such loving care in front of the child I once was. Anne's hair-brushing held that same intimacy, with a charming touch of self-admiration. When, I wondered, had she committed this outrage? Before she left? On the way? Or here in this small market town? I was later to find out that my last guess had been correct.

I thrust that sentence in her last letter far away, deep in my consciousness. The "accidentally" was cancelled out. Had Thame picked this sentence out? I felt that it must have struck a response in him, and yet, with wisdom, he had chosen to omit its evidence. And evidence it certainly was.

Why had she gone off with the individual she held in such contempt? "The man", as Thame dismissively called him, the man whom Anne, one night, had told me she could handle as she pleased. I remembered her "to use when and if". Had the moment presented itself as she, in a

81

panic about Maurice, decided to get away, coincided with the man and his car arriving at the opportune moment, to be used as a means of escape? I shall find out more, I thought, when I go the roadhouse and speak to Mrs. Stanley. Thame had given me a hint. The woman was a busybody, inquisitive. She would have noticed a lot, picked up a lot. Mrs. Stanley, I predicted, would tell me a great deal, too much perhaps. Mrs. Stanley was someone I would have to endure.

There was, of course, no need for me to know anything, reasonably speaking that is, but I was compelled by an inner mixture of pain and fury to add, to my intimate knowledge of Anne, experience of her which was not mine. I wondered where Maurice was. Did I want to question him? Such an encounter would have disconcerted both of us. We had been friends. We knew the score about each other. What truths would we have exchanged? How would the dialogue have gone? I have been your wife's lover, I could have said to him, but I wasn't in love with her, please understand that. Nor were you of course, I might have added. You just wanted a child and a cover. When it comes to it, I might have boasted, I was better for her than you. I used her as you did, but I did it less honestly, bringing tenderness and an illusion of love to make up for lack. Might I have lost my temper with him? Lost it because I was out of temper with myself? I could have berated him for his miserable self-pitying harassment, accused him of driving her to go off with a man she despised. Accused him of guilt for her suicide, taking the guilt I felt off myself. The conversation between Maurice and myself, had it taken place, would have been false, since we had both placed ourselves in a false position as far as Anne was concerned. Just as well, perhaps, that I was not given an opportunity to meet Maurice again. Just as well that I was never able to throw the blame on him. The blame, if blame there was in Anne's decision, Maurice and I had to share.

Later I heard that Maurice had resumed his journey to Spain, where, as you know, he more or less drank himself to death; an autopsy revealed cirrhosis of the liver. And the man? Back with his wife? Thame had told me that she had "glowered" at him throughout the inquest. I was happy to think that ultimately he had not got all his sums correct.

*

The next morning I went to the cemetery, clutching flowers I bought in the market square. Why is it, dear Francis, that we are driven to stand looking down at a plot of earth, with flowers in our hands, as a final gesture of love? Where did the bringing of flowers to the dead start? Not with the Greeks, if I remember rightly, who buried the hand of a suicide separately. Was this a Christian convention? This illogical act of casting blooms soon to decay as surely as the body buried under them was undergoing its inexorable process of disintegration. Flowers, a token of love, a token of mortality. And there I was with my token of mortality for Anne, the flowers of love which, throughout our lives, we throw so indiscriminately at our chosen ones of the moment, standing at her grave, knowing that my presence there was a final act of trust between us.

I had come, as I think she would have wished, to prove to myself that I would not turn away from the memory which I would hold safe and whole without distortion. When one is part of a group of mourners gathering around a newly dug grave, one is, in a sense, part of a ceremonial, which, because of the comfort of others, has an anaesthetic reaction on the shared grief. Alone, as I was, after the funeral, I could have been taken for a casual visitor in this small country cemetery, moving almost purposelessly from the ancient monuments of past centuries to the pitifully undignified allotment of recent burials. And there was Anne's, indistinguishable from its neighbours, with its faded flowers, and numbered temporary plaque freshly inscribed with name, dates of birth and death. I felt as

83

anonymous as her fast decaying flesh hidden in its coffin would soon be, leaving for evidence of life a few bones. What a barbaric action is burial; better far the annihilating cremation which does not leave the once living body to slow erosion of soil and vermin.

Such thoughts as these pressed as I stood, helpless in reaction, looking down on the consecrated ground which contained Anne's death. Her faith, in which I did not believe, had been taken into account, and I was glad of that for the sake of the feeling in her which subscribed to what had been for her some kind of anchorage. How resentful one is of all these rituals for the dead which can do nothing to revive the vibrant living being. This, I thought, is a nightmare. I shall wake up, put out my hand to the warm body beside me and, driven by a dream's panic, will make love to it. It was no nightmare, only a late autumn morning in the cemetery of a small town which did not match in any way the Anne I knew. She was so intensely metropolitan, so stylishly cosmopolitan, that I could place her, in my mind's eye, in all the capitals of the world and all the leisure places in the sun. Who would, in the future, come to this grave? And because on such occasions the sentiment in one is true, I mentally assured her memory of my love, an assurance I had denied her in life.

What I did with the rest of the day I cannot quite recall, probably there was nothing much to recall. I thought of going to the other hotel, to speak to Mrs. Stanley, but I was exhausted, emotionally I daresay, and could only potter about the street of that small market town, returning to my hotel to rest through the afternoon. Thame would be coming to take me out to dinner, I reminded myself before I fell asleep.

★

Thame wore a grey suit which struck me as rather festive. We drove, in his car, to a road-house out of town. I told him I had been to the cemetery.

"You know," I said, "it was very kind of you to manage your report so that she should have a Catholic burial. It mattered to her, her religion, I mean."

He did not exactly deny that. "Well, we have to use our judgement in such matters. She had been taking a hell of a lot of pills for a very long time. Under stress people can take that extra and tip the balance."

I told him I was going to see Mrs. Stanley the following day.

"You don't have to believe everything she tells you." Thame's dry note was very evident. "She's apt to stretch a point." Then unexpectedly: "We shall never really know what did happen that night, shall we? We can only hazard a guess."

"You suspect something unusual?" I noted the hint in his voice.

"Let's say," metaphorically he stretched himself, "let's say there was a row. I'd guess there had been a row all those three days. Why did he bunk? Fear of his wife? Don't think so, entirely. She must know him pretty well. False name registered. Usual in such cases. It doesn't make sense – the bunk, I mean."

"Perhaps he'd had enough?" I spoke gently.

"What had he had?" Thame placed the question squarely before us. "He wasn't her kind." He spoke with conviction.

"What makes you think so?" I asked.

"Well I did a bit of investigation into her past." He then tried to put the matter delicately. "They were all more her age, her class. She was an educated woman, cultured, she had taste." He looked at me.

It was the second time he had allowed himself a personal remark. At our previous dinner he had, almost flatly, told me that of all the people, witnesses, he had seen in this affair he liked me. Had I, unconsciously, flirted with him? You once told me, Francis – I must confess, to my utter astonishment – that I could not resist trying to charm people. A distasteful idea to me, since it reminded me of my mother's quite frankly expressed charm act.

I parried the implication.

"She was young, young," I said lightly. "I mean to me. I'm almost ten years older."

"That family of hers, I couldn't make them out. Indifferent lot. She didn't appear to belong to them."

I explained that a godmother had more or less taken on Anne's education, and gave him the background of the French convent and the cultural establishment in Florence.

"Yes, so I was told," he said. "Nor were they much interested in the child. Treated her as some sort of burden."

"Are you always so thorough in your investigations?" I asked rather tartly.

"The case interested me," he said flatly.

Indeed, Francis, I could feel his interest like a physical fact.

"She had a rotten life, on the whole," he said. "You were the only one to care." His mild statement made me catch my breath. "They all used her. I don't like that at all."

"She'd have liked you," I said, simply because he had used Anne's account of those in her past.

"Oh, I'm a dull chap."

Then he went on to tell me about himself. For quite a while he spread his childhood and youth before me. It held the happiness of love, especially for the Shropshire countryside. His father had been a farmer and, for a time, he had expected to follow in his footsteps.

"I read a lot. I was interested in people, still am," he explained.

This interest in people had led him to the police force, fortuitously, through the influence of a local Inspector who was one of his father's pals. A note of indifference crept in when he spoke of his "settling down" with his practical wife.

"I miss that country life – sometimes. But I like my work. It brings me in touch with people."

How out of touch, I wondered, was he with that practical wife who ran all his domestic arrangements, including strict family planning. How strange that such a man, with such potentials in understanding, should be land-locked in that small market town.

"Tragic, tragic, that this should happen to such a beautiful young woman." He returned to that. "I'd say she was happy with you."

Then he asked a strange question. "Do you make people happy?"

"Well, I try. Don't we all?"

"No. Few of us do – or can. I think you could make . . ." he broke off abruptly. "Would you care to dance?"

There was a small floor-space for this purpose. The music was piped. Some tension about him made me agree. For a big man he danced rather well, and I told him so. He held me more tightly than I had expected. It was not unpleasant, just inappropriate. I put on my act of chatter-box so as to break the sexuality I felt in him. The image of his practical wife flicked through my mind, so evidently a censoring element in his life.

"Do you only like women?" His question came almost in spite of himself.

"Oh, I'm madly catholic!" I made it sound as jazzy as possible as we returned to our table. "And rather tired." I knew he would accept this code as a refusal.

Something in my relationship with Anne – and in the idea of Anne he had built up in his mind – touched his dormant sensuality, inspired his report to come down on her side. My presence was a catalyst to his emotional confusion. I suddenly appreciated that he was giving me more time than was, officially, necessary. I brought us back to previous matter.

"I wonder why she went off with that particular man. She could have chosen better." I wished to sound cynical.

"No, he wasn't her kind," he repeated.

"Even so, she came away with him." I was returning to my doubting-Thomas attitude towards Anne.

Thame looked at me as though I had disappointed him. "He happened to come along when she wanted to get away. That type always appears at the wrong moment."

87

Inwardly I thought that Thame and Father Luke would get on splendidly together, in that both ever reached for the best in others.

Doggedly Thame continued. "He posed as a protector. There she was, harassed by that sick husband, trapped with her uncaring family, not knowing where to turn."

I interrupted. "I tried to persuade her to come to me."

He ignored this. "He knew the score. He'd witnessed the matrimonial fights. Just think, can't you see it all?" He briefly touched my hand. "There she is, frantic. She wants to get away. It's his chance. She wants out, but not on his terms. I think she must have made that clear. And he'd agree. Yes, he'd agree to anything at that stage. Once away with him, she was compromised, caught. There were the rows, you know."

"You've a vivid imagination," I flicked at him.

"And what does your imagination tell you? Tell me that. You knew her."

What indeed did my imagination tell me? At that stage I was holding it back, facing only what facts I could pick up. Time enough to correlate these later.

"I sometimes think," I said, because his urgency required an answer, "that I didn't know her at all."

He was not having anything to do with my denial of knowledge.

"You mean it wasn't like her to −" he hesitated "− to be careless with the pills?"

"In some circumstances," I conceded, "it is possible to imagine. Yet now I don't really know what I think." I stopped myself from adding that surely sleeping with yet another man, if she had, was hardly unusual enough to warrant a suicidal gesture. "There must have been a reason."

Thame made me, with his roundabout comments and personal interest in me, put my finger on it. There must have been a reason. It was the reason which had brought me to this small market town. A lover's first instinct when confronted by contrary behaviour. Why?

Thame was telling me more about the man. He had gone to some trouble to find out all he could. A fairly wealthy man who lived half the year abroad: for tax purposes, Thame assumed. He called himself a property speculator, which occupation appeared to bring out Thame's distaste for all work that was in any way devious. A wife who matched him and suited him, a woman predominantly concerned with money and social position. "No love lost between them." Thame drew his own conclusions. That she knew of his obsession about Anne, she had admitted to Thame.

"She'd watched it for years," Thame said. "Watched him being turned down time and again. He told me."

I could see that Thame had been rough in his examination of the man.

"Hadn't the decency to let her alone. Waited until she was in a jam."

Had he, I wondered, made clear his contempt during the questioning? I rather thought he had.

"She must have had lovely hair before she cut it off," he said.

So, Thame had picked that one up, I thought. Our eyes met and held each other's for a few moments. Something in his gave me a clue, or shall we say pushed me to a fanciful theory: Anne had arrested his attention; dead and with shorn locks, she struck him as beautiful. His "I only saw her naked" had initially lead me astray. I had immediately associated it with the image in my mind of a dead body on the morgue slab. Probably Thame's reference went no further than the sight of Anne still in that hotel bed.

Then because this soft-spoken man, this superficially ordinary man with his country background, his reading, his interest in people, his practical wife and his adolescent daughters, was, as it were, opening himself to me, almost engaging my trust, I gave him a confidence, as a sort of comfort.

"She never, you know, made the running. She was just there, to be used."

I saw him almost think this one out. Then he said:

"You mean in the past?"

Again, I awarded him full marks for perception. Because the moment was too raw, in the sense that we were neither of us ready to look at its totality, being still in the area of strangers to each other, by common unspoken consent we back-tracked into general exchanges and political opinions. He contributed a number of anecdotes relating to some of his past cases, less searing than the one we both held in our minds. He was not, it was evident, a man for punishment. His attitude was that, in general, people were in trouble through frustrating circumstances or personal inadequacies.

"The blame, you know," he said, "should be shared." He sighed. "However there are regulations which determine decisions. Judgement I try to withhold."

Had he, I asked, any interest in moving to a metropolitan area?

"None at all." He explained. "It's the same thing really, aggravated in cities. People in this quiet part of the world, if pushed, would act with a sameness." Then, unconsciously giving me his motivation. "Here it's easier to help them. They haven't been brutalised so much."

He told me the story of an adolescent who had knifed his grandmother to death with repeated and vicious stabs. The lad, Thame said, although "a bit thick", was well treated, relatively content with his lot. It had taken Thame some time to discover the reason, which, as he pointed out was so simple. The grandmother had had the youth's cat put to sleep, really out of kindness because the animal was old and frail.

"It was something he loved," Thame said.

Back at my hotel he saw me to the door.

"I'm busy tomorrow," he said. "But I'll drop in on you about nine, after you've seen Mrs. Stanley. By the way," he added, "my name's Roger."

★

I telephoned Mrs. Stanley the next morning and arranged to drive out to her place in the afternoon. My prepared explanation that I was a friend of Anne, shocked by the tragic news, was brushed aside with: "Ah yes, you want to know all what happened." The voice was nastily bright, a trifle common in accent, and rather more confidential than I thought my mild explanation warranted. I anticipated no good from that voice, and resolved to be cautious, then realised that, since my name had been mentioned at the inquest, she was able to place me immediately.

It was an Edwardian type of small mansion house, a typical "private" hotel for chance passers-by, some few miles out of the town, reasonably well-kept. It offered meals and drinks to the motorist on his way elsewhere. There was little to be said for it really. Why would anyone stay here, I asked myself as I walked into the reception area, flanked on one side by a small lounge, with a bar opposite. Dead-tired and not within any distance of one's ultimate destination one might, in desperation, book in for a bed and a meal. My hotel in town was pure luxury compared to this nothingness.

Mrs. Stanley was a crisp middle-aged woman, dressed in a jersey and skirt, with a perfectly horrid necklace of what looked like assorted bones hanging round her neck. Hair peroxided to a tight glitter, mean little features held in control, and eyes, pale blue, glinting anticipatory pleasure at me. She was keenly excited, yet held it at bay, since, after all, we were meeting on an occasion of tragedy.

"Come into my sitting-room," she said. "You'll want some tea? My husband is resting. He's not too strong. Frankly I do most of the running of this place. He looks after the bar."

The way she said all this told me quite a lot about their married life. A maid appeared with a tray. It had all been planned. Mrs. Stanley was out to enjoy her afternon tea. I conquered my aversion and instinct to flee by saying how kind it was of her to receive me.

"My dear," she said, "nothing like that ever happened before in this house. It shook me up, I can tell you. It all fell on me of course. My husband won't interest himself." Again a glimpse into her marriage. "He sees nothing. I am the one who notices. I've had to be. And, I can tell you, little escapes me."

I clucked hypocritically in sympathy.

"You come from London?" I nodded as she went on: "I'd have liked to live in London. This isn't what I was used to. Not what I expected. Still, it's a nice little property. Should anything happen to my better half" – she gave a false chuckle – "I'll sell it and off I'll be to Barnes. Do you know Barnes? I lived there as a child. Lovely place Barnes, only a hop away from town."

I was fast getting her picture. Had she any family? I tentatively enquired.

"Well, no. My hubby is much, oh much older than I am. Anyway children are never grateful. I'm better off without." Rapidly she was giving me her life story. "I might, you know, go to Torquay."

"Torquay?" I had lost the thread.

"When it happens." She gave another chuckle and nodded at the ceiling. "Upstairs. Torquay is a lovely place you know. Fashionable."

She was expecting her husband's demise at any moment, and she had her emergency plans ready for action.

"Your name was mentioned at the inquest." The way she said it sounded like an accusation.

I acknowledged the fact.

"I know I shouldn't say it but in my opinion the police mishandled the whole thing. They should have gone deeper. I told that Thame, 'There's more in this than meets the eye.' But trust a firsthand witness, oh no, that's not their way. All they want to do is sweep everything under the carpet." She looked indignant. "I was hardly able to give my evidence properly. All they wanted they said was facts. Facts! That Thame wouldn't know one when it was under his nose. A slow man, not up to it,

92

that's what I think. I knew something was brewing from the time they arrived." She meant Anne and the man.

I encouraged her to expand. Her way of telling her story was gruesome, gruesome in the relish she so clearly derived from it. According to Mrs. Stanley, as soon as Anne and the man arrived, she, Mrs. Stanley, had not been, as she put it, "happy" about them, recollecting in retrospect a presentiment of disaster which had not been hers at the time.

"They registered as man and wife." She assumed an expression of shocked morality, stressing her worldliness in such matters by a "Ha!" which indicated her ability to nose out a falsehood.

"He looked old enough to be her father," she wildly exaggerated. "You know, don't you, that it was her name, her married name and her address that he wrote in the book?" She knew I did not know. "That's how we traced her family." She spoke as though she, and not Thame, had done the routine work.

They were on their way to Cornwall she said, adding, "At least that's what he said."

Anne, apparently, had said nothing. She looked ill, Mrs. Stanley recalled, and wore dark glasses. That was a fact I recognised.

"She wore them most of the time." Mrs. Stanley clearly thought this sinister. "Even at dinner. She didn't eat much, or drink."

The man had done all the talking. Anne had appeared indifferent. He it was who commented on the room.

"It's perfect here, isn't it, darling?" he had said to Anne. "You can rest here."

He had then explained to Mrs. Stanley that his wife had not been well, was in need of rest and quiet.

"He was the nervy one," Mrs. Stanley said. "She was quite calm. Mind you" – she gave a little nod – "she was boss. He was under her thumb."

"In what way?" I butted in.

"Well she did what she liked with him. Sent him out of their room to the bar. Left him to eat alone. Ignored him.

93

Hardly listened to him when he spoke to her. The next day she went out by herself. Ordered a taxi to take her into town. He wanted to stop her. Couldn't of course. When she came back she'd had all her hair cut off – well, cut short that is. Pity that. Pretty hair she had and what a colour. Even my hubby remarked on it." She moved nearer to me. "You know they changed rooms?"

I became alert. I knew she was about to tell me something I would rather have not known, yet which I had to know.

"Yes, the next day. When she was out in the afternoon. He came and asked for a change." Mrs. Stanley positively sparkled with suppressed malice. They had a room with two single beds. He changed it to one with a double bed."

I kept a tight hold on my expression.

She gave a coarse laugh. "It didn't help much. The next day he went out on his own. Said she wasn't well. Be that as it may, she came downstairs after he'd gone, sat on the verandah with a pot of tea I brought her."

I could imagine how Mrs. Stanley had attempted to use this opportunity for gaining information. Anne, according to Mrs. Stanley, looked sad. Mrs. Stanley could see that something was worrying her, because Anne had temporarily laid aside her dark glasses.

"Beautiful eyes, yes, I must say she had beautiful eyes. But of course she'd been taking all those drugs, and you know they make the pupils bright and large."

That she had not got far with conversation was clear. She excused her failure with:

"Well, I didn't want to worry her. She had enough on her plate. I could see that."

So Mrs. Stanley observed from a distance, puzzled that Anne picked up none of the magazines she had helpfully brought to her.

"Just staring into space," she said, then dramatically: "Thinking about it. What she did that night."

"That night?" I steered her talk.

"He dined alone. She locked herself in their room."

94

She then explained that she happened to be in the corridor when the man had tried the door, found it locked, and was about to bang on the door, when he saw Mrs. Stanley hovering, and went downstairs to the bar. According to Mrs. Stanley's hubby he drank a lot.

"They had a lot of rows," she said.

I interrupted to point out that, from what she had so far told me, they had been singularly silent.

"Not when they were alone," she was triumphant. "I have to be everywhere. See that everything's done properly in this place, so I heard them quarrelling that first night, and the second one." Regretfully she admitted that she had not caught many of the words exchanged. "But she had a quiet voice." I wondered how near the door Mrs. Stanley had stood. She had had one success in her eavesdropping; she had heard him say, "Well, you've buggered that up now, haven't you?"

During the late evening of the third day, the man had gone upstairs, then rushed into the kitchen asking for coffee for his wife. Mrs. Stanley had offered to take it up. He insisted on taking it up himself.

At this point Mrs. Stanley let her imagination run riot.

"She could have been on her way out then. He could have thrown in some more pills, finished her off. I told that Thame this. He said the coffee hadn't been touched. How would he know? He didn't analyse it."

"Why should he want to finish her off?" I had to know what had put this into her mind.

She hedged a bit. "Well, she wasn't much good to him was she? I heard him say" – another bit of eavesdropping – "a man could kill you."

This woman was grim. The whole place was grim. Anne here, I could hardly believe it, I did not want to believe it, yet here I was sitting next to this mean-spirited woman whose equally mean-spirited life welcomed the tragedy of Anne as some exciting event, and would, doubtless, regale herself with the memory in the future, adding fresh detail to her account each time she told it.

I wanted to get away from her presence, yet could not do so until she had exhausted her fund of information and comment. Realising that at this stage of her story she required encouragement, I muttered something on the lines of what a shock she must have had.

She brightened considerably as she went on to tell me that shortly after taking up the coffee, the man had rushed downstairs again. "Distraught," she said. "He must have a doctor he said. His wife was very ill."

Mrs. Stanley asked if she could go up. "Please do," he said. As though he could have stopped her.

"And that was the last time, before the inquest," she stressed the drama – "that I saw him. He was out and off before you could count ten."

It was the peak of excitement for her that night. So before the doctor arrived, Mrs. Stanley went into Anne's room.

"She was lying so neatly," Mrs. Stanley repeated the words. "So neatly. Beautifully fitted out in her black nightie." It crossed my mind that I had never known what Anne wore in bed. "With her hands outside the bed-clothes, fingers stretched, mouth open, eyes closed." Mrs. Stanley's recollection was vivid. "I saw then that she was really beautiful. I opened her eyes, and saw she'd taken some drugs. I lifted her head and put my arm under her pillow to lift her and found three letters."

She had it word perfect. I guessed this was her solo performance at the inquest. She never knew how near I was to hitting her, not her precisely, rather the picture she drew. I must have closed my eyes for a few seconds. When I opened them she was peering avidly at me.

"Were they yours?" she asked.

"Yes," I said, in a tone that brooked no further comment from her. I knew full well that she knew, because, before the doctor arrived, Mrs. Stanley must have gratified her curiosity and read the letters.

She had waited for this moment, and I could not stop her as she rushed into what, clearly, she had been saving up for me during all our conversation.

"I had a close woman friend, you know. My hubby didn't approve. Said she was an interfering bitch. Nothing like that, of course, between us. Oh no, nothing nasty!" She was freewheeling with relish. "I've always wondered – you'll forgive my asking, won't you? But, what exactly do they do? Of course," she regained self-control, "I'm not suggesting that . . ." She had trouble completing her sentence. "I had to read the letters, you know. I mean, we had to know about her. Of course, you're a writer. They said so in court. Used to flowery language. I was quite struck. Writers exaggerate, I suppose? Did you mean? I mean they were rather passionate. That's to say intimate. My hubby can't write the simplest letter. Grace – that was my friend – used to write to me, but she did go on about her ailments and her cat."

I was not able to stop the flow. I just looked at her with as much contempt as I could reveal in my expression. Evidently this got through to her, and I was amused to note that she was now looking nervously at me. Her manner became conciliatory.

"The letters?" My tone was ice.

"The police, that Thame, took them away, with her handbag."

There was nothing more to be said. As she escorted me to the entrance, she asked me whether I would like to see the room. Need I add I avoided answering, and drove away as fast as I could.

★

I had gone there for information and had been given my fill of it. I had, in some ways, gained further knowledge of Anne's last day. I had also been presented with another puzzle which I would find difficult to unravel, and which, at that moment, it was desperately urgent for me to make my mind up about. Yes, dear Francis, I was as shaky as the next lover, as obsessively concentrated, near to jealousy, as I worked out the implication of their changing rooms from one with two single beds to one with a double bed.

One might say that such a speculation was undignified when related to the occasion. She was dead; what did it matter? I know that you, the seeker after motive, will fully understand how this new fact unhinged me and became an importunate irritant which I could not get out of my mind. It boiled down, quite simply, to whether or not the man had become Anne's lover on one of those nights. Or on both.

I think that most probably, if this did happen, it was on the second night. The first booking of a room with two beds would suggest that Anne had perhaps struck an understanding with him that he should keep his place. At least you will allow the probability of this prognosis. They arrived as man and wife, were shown to a room with two beds, and Anne, at that stage, would hardly have protested without revealing the falsity of their registration. In any case, that first night she was tired, sought rest. It vaguely adds up, does it not? Although I admit that a single bed is no barrier to a lover. He had the rooms changed when she had gone out to get her hair cut short. What could she say by way of protest? Assuming she felt inclined to protest. There was Mrs. Stanley's conviction that "she was boss". If this was true, the room could have been changed back again. That is if she had the will to do so. There was her passivity in matters arranged for her.

My probing went straight to the room with the double bed. A man, frustrated by years of siege, given the opportunity at long last, determined to get some change out of the business. A woman, Anne, habituated by her past to a certain acquiescence in sexual matters, clearly at odds with herself, an easy target really. It did not seem possible that the sharing of the double bed was without sexuality. That he would certainly have, as they say, thrust his attentions on her, would appear to be within the realm of fact.

"She was boss." Mrs. Stanley's phrase came back, linking itself to Anne's hardness of tone when I had previously questioned her about him after that dinner at the Connaught ("Do you think I can't control a man?") and established a doubt for me.

You will note that my doubt then was on Anne's side. He was not the type for rape. He was too self-conscious socially, witness his refraining from banging on the locked door when he saw Mrs. Stanley hovering in the corridor. I wonder, how this little puzzle would be solved if it were yours. More clear-cut I imagine than my approach. "Sex, my dear Cass." Your masculine verdict would be crisp. I could parry and qualify your judgement (assuming you made it so direct), remembering that I had always intuitively felt that Anne assumed a passive role with her past lovers, and thereby was able to convince myself that the running, as it were, was all his. Whatever happened or did not happen had hardly produced any joy. He had taken himself off the whole of the following day. She had stayed in the room until he left. Another of Mrs. Stanley's remarks came to mind, the fruit of her eavesdropping, his "You've buggered that up now." What had she "buggered up"?

There was a threat in it, a blackmail lurking. It suggested she had compromised herself. By being in that hotel with him? Had he known about me? Had he found the letters in her handbag, including hers written to me? My imagination rushed towards the explanations. Was it possible that she had taunted him with her love for me? Mrs. Stanley had mentioned the rows, and so had Thame. What were the rows about? Had he – you see how I can stretch a conjecture – had he hinted that if I knew they were lovers – and by going away with him, sharing the same hotel room, created at least circumstantial evidence to be taken into consideration – I would, as it were, cut and run? Would I have believed him or believed her? "You've buggered that up now" could be so explained. And the second result of Mrs. Stanley's eavesdropping, "A man could kill you." Why? What for? At what time was Mrs. Stanley standing outside their room when these words were spoken? I wished now I had questioned her

99

about that. This was on the second night, the night of the double bed. Why does a man kill, or wish to do so, the woman he desires? When? When she mocks him? When she turns away? When she repulses him? When she shows him, afterwards, in what contempt she holds him?

★

When Thame came, later that evening, I could have thrown myself in his arms for comfort. He gave me one of his reflective looks. "So she upset you, did she, Mrs. S.?"

I gave him the picture of my grim encounter, then I asked. "Did he, the man, know about me?"

"I think so." Thame knew I had a reason for the question. "He first told me your name meant nothing to him. Then he hedged. Eventually he admitted knowing you as her friend." The stress on the "eventually" put by Thame made me smile as I again saw how ruthlessly he had dealt with the man. "He denied knowing about the letters. Then he tripped himself up when he said that he was astonished to find her passport in her handbag. I reckon he's the type to pry."

I had another question for him. "Did you know they changed rooms?"

His whole being understood the question. "Yes, I brought it up."

We were in a very delicate area.

"That, Cass," he used my Christian name for the first time, "is something we shall never know, for certain."

I felt we shared a common distress about this uncertainty.

"For what it's worth," he continued, "the post-mortem revealed no evidence of sexual intercourse."

"But," I said quickly, "she was found late on the third night, which he spent in the bar." Then, irrelevantly: "How beastly post-mortems are."

"Yes, but informative. The pathologist's key word is recent, that's to say within a forty-eight hour period." He then added with his policeman's caution, "More or less." Then reverted to a previous remark of the previous evening: "He wasn't her type, you know."

Nor, I thought, are you a doubting Thomas. I gave a small laugh as I looked at this steady man who presented such an image of imperturbability, yet, even he, with his confessed weakness, his personal interest, had been seduced to speculate when his brief instructed him only to report.

"Did she lie then?" he suddenly asked.

"She said she didn't," I replied, not adding "to me".

I told him about Mrs. Stanley's riotous imagination about the man spilling more tablets into the coffee. Thame laughed, said it was typical of Mrs. S. No evidence at all. The coffee was not touched.

"Someone in the habit of taking drugs, a lot of them, could be driven to take more." Thame gave his sentence a pause. "In defiance."

He had given me another mental picture to nag at. Had Anne threatened to take an overdose, the man disbelieving, thereby egging her on, in temper, to swallow more than she had intended?

Rather ruefully Thame said, "Pity Mrs. Stanley wasn't more successful in her spying. We might have a clearer idea, about the rows I mean. He denied them. Called Mrs. S. a malicious bitch, said she'd made it up, then rather contradicted that by saying that Anne" – Thame used her Christian name for the first time – "that she would scream at him when he tried to reason with her. Did what Mrs. S. overhear strike you as possible?"

"Very much so," I said.

I sensed the growing intimacy between us.

"Have you been married?" he asked.

I shook my head. Some instinct made me expect his next question.

"Men in your life?" he tried to make it light-hearted.

"Now and then." Then, I added as an intentional irritant. "I'm rather restless. I don't settle down easily."

Ruefully, I thought of my twenty years spent with one person.

"You're trying to put me off." He half-scowled.

"Well yes, you're already too much involved. Don't you think?"

"How much did you care? About her I mean?"

"Christ! What a question! And why do you want to know?" Something in his tone prevented my asking what right he assumed.

"Say it's just personal interest." His smile disarmed my anger. "I like you."

"Why do you like me?" I was fierce with him.

"I'm getting to know you."

"Oh, for God's sake." I brushed the intimacy aside. "How much did I care? You want to know? I didn't really care at all, in the beginning. Just sex." I threw it at him. "You're a romantic. I can smell a romantic a mile away. Why? Because, in my fashion, at times in my life, I'm a romantic too. Not in this case though. She irritated me, then amused me, or rather brought the worst out in me. And, if you really want to know, I needed some fuel for my vanity. It was at a low ebb. Not nice, is it? You can't take that."

"You push yourself hard, don't you?" His tone was mild.

"I have to when I consider the result of some of my actions. Oh, all right, it did change. Will that satisfy your sentimentality? I became what is known as vaguely infatuated. Though perhaps that's too strong an emphasis. I luxuriated in her – luxuriated in her love for me. Beastly way of going on, wouldn't you say? Habit, you know, breeds tenderness, a sort of love. A counterfeit. Towards the end I almost wanted to make her happy."

"Were you happy?"

"Why do you insist?"

"I'm trying to understand. To understand you. I would have said, from the little I know of you, that you don't go in for casual affairs." It was more question than statement.

I decided to be rough with him. "On the contrary, I'm expert with casual affairs. Dammit, you make me say this

102

kind of thing. Do you really want to know the truth about me? I despise casual affairs. Don't misunderstand me. I've had my share. And pretty annoyed with myself afterwards I've been."

"That's what I thought," he sounded almost complacent.

"There was something unutterably sad about her, underneath all the polish," I said. "I think it touched my heart." Then to punish him for his questions. "She was very good in bed."

We looked at each other, both knowing that, casually speaking, we could have drifted into an unreal situation. A situation I saved us from by smiling, almost lovingly, at him, as I said:

"I'm quite diffident, you know, when it comes to the real thing. I suspect you are too. We don't make first moves, do we? Not if it really matters. How absurd we are. Rushing in when it's of no account, holding back when it's deep and true. What a lot of time fools like us waste. Have you got the picture now?"

"Thoroughly," he placed his hand on mine, and got up to leave, having work to finish by the morning.

"Look," he said. "I'm off tomorrow. Thought of having a day in the country. Why don't you join me?"

★

And there I was, dear Francis, absurdly committed to a day in the country with this not quite orthodox Coroner's police officer, absurd for being almost out of character with my reason for being there. What was my reason for being there? In that small market town which took no notice of my presence, simply because I was not part of it. Walking the streets and pacing round the square, I had a sensation of not quite being there, some ghostly drifter, purposeless.

I thought about my London life. About my friends, my work, my decision, still to make, about my future before

Adrian returned to his own house. Perhaps, it crossed my mind, I would go and stay with Rick for a while. That might help me find my bearings. Rick, with his association with my youth, was a landmark from my past which had endured. Our long *amitié amoureuse* dated back to that time when I still felt security in the background my mother had provided. With Rick I could chatter about those jazzy near-innocent days, when I followed in mother's haphazard decisions to drag me and my stepfather from rented villas to hotels carefully chosen for their eagerness to cater for her every whim. Rick himself had experience of just such a background in adolescence. Our shared memories would, or might, enable me take stock, and, perhaps, reach some conclusions.

I had been driven to this town by the force of love, however you define love, which too often is regarded of secondary interest by a world racked with violence and social conflict. An account of love, which is the account I am relating to you, is often considered of limited peripheral worth in the wider scheme of universal considerations, which, of course, have no place in this story of Anne, which in no way is a denial of concern with them. You wanted to know what happened, and what happened was Anne, and my account of her must be substantially subjective, because so much in her past, which made her the woman I knew, was to me hearsay, and equally subjective, coming as it mostly did from her words. Now, at this final stage of my story of Anne, there was Thame, Roger Thame, a man who viewed Anne through his harvest of conflicting facts and his imagination. It was this quality in him, his imagination, which made me respond to his invitation. It is a quality sadly lacking in this troubled world.

★

As I waited for Thame to arrive the next morning, I thought of my last day with Anne, when we also had enjoyed a day out in the country. That had been at the beginning of September when summer warmth was still reflected by the sun. Today, equally bright in sunlight, the flavour was definitely autumnal. October with the onset of winter was only round the corner.

Thame (I could never think of him as Roger) was adept at getting us clear of the town to a prospect of hills, woods and fields. The countryman in him had a quick eye for signs of wild life, and there was great pleasure in his enthusiasm. I matched his knowledge by telling him about the years I had spent in Switzerland in childhood and adolescence.

"You and I," I said, "had happy childhoods. Unfortunate in a way. Things are never as perfect afterwards."

"Perhaps not." He was reluctant to admit this.

"Mind you" – I wished to thank him for his care of me – "at least we can appreciate all the happy days when they come along, such as this one."

"She had some happy days?" His was a tentative question. We were back to Anne.

"I think so, yes." I decided to be decisive. "Some very happy days." I sensed my words pleased him.

Was it true? I asked myself this, as I listened to Thame giving me some more nature notes. How could I really tell? One day, yes, in Thame's view of happiness. The day in the country, my last day with her, had given her an impression of happiness enjoyed, simply because of the length of hours we spent together. How could I tell Thame about the evenings, the nights, the sessions of love? Did they add up to happiness as he understood this? I rather thought not. His understanding of happiness did not hold that kind of pleasure, yet he could anticipate it, imaginatively almost touch it.

I decided to please him further. "I think the first years of the marriage, well the first one, were rather happy. She enjoyed the travel. They did a lot of that."

"Restless, yes, I can understand she was restless," he said.

"She was searching," I explained. "Searching for what we can never really find."

105

"What?" He was brusque.

That was a question. What do people search for? Security? Love? The latter often cancels out the former. It would hardly do to be cyncial with Thame, so I compromised.

"Oh miracles, I suppose."

He returned to that later as we sat in a country pub eating bread and cheese and drinking very strong local cider.

"Had she found what she was searching for?" he asked.

It was a leading question and I was not sure how to handle it.

"You're obsessed by her," I said.

"By her?" The look he gave me was too definite to be mistaken. His obsession took me in as well.

"Had she?" he repeated.

"In some way perhaps," was all I was prepared to admit.

"Yes," he spoke softly. "I can see why." Then continued in his normal tone. "It struck me, you know, through all the evidence," he said, "that it was a mistake."

"You mean an accident?"

"No, let's not quibble about that. The dose was too massive. No, an error of judgement. Her decision to go off with the man, that was the accident." He was anxious to express himself precisely, and failed as we all do when faced with a dilemma. He was blunt. "She had found what she was searching for. She didn't want to throw it away. By going away with the man she was putting it at risk."

I was rather startled by his bringing it out into the open. He had read the letters. He had accepted my relationship with Anne as one of his facts.

"Then why" — I slapped it down between us — "did she kill herself?" You tell me, I thought, you tell me.

"Well, Cass" — he spoke gently — "as I see it, from what facts we have at our disposal, and from what we know about her, it could have been guilt. Self-disgust too. She'd committed, well, let's say an outrage against herself, that's if she did. Bearing in mind the pathologist's report." He paused. "How could she explain the man? To you?"

"So the double bed was circumstantial evidence?" I was sharp.

"Circumstantial yes, not substantive."

"Oh God!" I lost my temper. "It was nothing to her. A man more or less. Of little account."

"So circumstantial evidence counts with you?" He was smiling.

"What about you? What do you think?" I nearly added: "With your idealised view of Anne."

"He wasn't her kind." He returned to that as to a lodestar. Then, slyly for him. "Did she know you were apt to believe circumstantial evidence?"

He had scored a point. Ruefully I smiled, acknowledging my weakness and Anne's experience of it. How often had I doubted most of what she told me? More often out of habit, often when not doubting her at all. Thame put another picture in my mind. A view of what explanations I would have demanded if Anne had returned on the day stated in her letter. What would she have told me? "I never lie to you," she had said. Would she have told me the whole truth or part of it? It would have taken some telling. I could see myself on an occasion that could now never be, positively tormenting her with my frantic need to be told nothing but the truth. The very thought filled me with horror, horror at that in myself for which there was no justification, even for a lover. In my place Thame would not have questioned her, that I knew. He would have allowed her to forget an incident, if there had been such an incident, which might have worried her. He was kinder than I was.

A new feeling existed between Thame and myself. A sense of relief in me that I had no need to prevaricate with him. I could be myself with him. Previously I had hovered in some false position, not consciously so, merely because I was not entirely certain as to how Thame wished to view my position in all this. Now I knew I was part of his obsession, to which he brought his imaginative concept. Because of that personal interest of his, I came in for a degree of protection. I guessed that his invitation to share his "day off" was part of this concern.

★

Dear Francis, I can see, on the tip of your tongue, the question? Did my relationship with Thame veer towards any intimacy? That indeed would set a dramatic seal on this story of Anne, and I am almost tempted to tease you with some ambiguity. Only one moment could be so described.

Late in the afternoon, as we stood at a fence looking down at the village where he had promised me a farmhouse tea, the peace was shattered by a chilling scream. It was a hare caught by some marauding animal, probably a stoat, Thame thought. We had a quick view of some body streaking away. It was over so quickly, although the echo of the scream remained about us. I closed my eyes, and instinctively clung to Thame, who held me for a few minutes. It could have been the moment your unasked question anticipated. There was so much between us, so much of Anne. His face was near mine. He was not unattractive, and I liked him. It could so easily have been possible. He was more ready than I. He wanted protection from his curious personal involvement as much as I did, possibly more so, since his personal interest had surprised something deep in his nature. I touched his face with as much gentleness as I felt, and said:

"No, Roger, you can't know her this way."

"I wasn't thinking entirely about her," he said.

I kissed his cheek and then, to thank him for much, I gave him Anne's words to me, spoken at another time.

"It's been a beautiful day, a beautiful day."

The rest of our day together could be described as one spent in loving friendship, in easy exchanges about our separate lives and our articles of faith about the world we shared. To enumerate these would be useless padding; I mention it only to stress the rapport between us. During those last hours, until late evening, when he left me at my hotel, we knew each other as much as any of us know our friends, although it was clear, an anomaly in fact, that we would never meet again, corresponding briefly, if at all. I told him I was going home the next day, and he said he would pop in during the morning to say goodbye.

He came towards midday, and we had a drink together. No word about Anne was spoken by either of us. He was with me barely half an hour.

"You must look after yourself in the future," he said. "Think the best you can about all this." It was his farewell to me.

Just before he stood up to go, he drew from an inner pocket an envelope and gave it to me. I knew what it contained, and, when, after he left, I opened it, the contents were what I had intuitively expected – my three letters to Anne found under her pillow. Now no longer on the shelf but in my hands.

other recent fiction from GMP:

Agustin Gomez-Arcos
THE CARNIVOROUS LAMB
translated by William Rodarmor

Into a shuttered house in Franco's Spain, where the ghosts of past rebellion and present defeat still taint the air, Ignacio is born, the carnivorous lamb of the title. His father stays locked in his study, amid memories of political failure. His mother, vague but implacable ruler of her shadowy domain, refuses to acknowledge her son's existence. Only his brother Antonio is real – father-surrogate, teacher, protector and eventual lover. Their relationship is the centre of this story of one family's suffocation under an intolerable regime, which is also an incisive, savagely funny, but not entirely despairing look at post-Civil War Spain.

Born in 1939, Agustin Gomez-Arcos has been living in France since 1968. Before his exile from Spain, he received the Lope de Vega Prize for two of his plays and was widely acclaimed for his translations from French. Despite this, his works were banned and he left the country. *The Carnivorous Lamb*, written in French, appeared in 1975 and received the Prix Hermès for the best novel of that year.

"A carnal poem, frank, provocative, triumphant ... and a dirge for Spain" – *Le Monde*.

"Extraordinary, beautifully constructed. Agustin Gomez-Arcos extends and deepens his sexual themes until we realise that the entire bizarre tale is a metaphor for the future of Spain" – *San Francisco Chronicle*.

ISBN 0 85449 018 3 (paperback)
0 85449 019 1 (cloth)

Edward Lucie-Smith
THE DARK PAGEANT

In the confusion of fifteenth-century France, with the kingdom riven between the King of England, the Duke of Burgundy and the still uncrowned Dauphin, two romantic figures stand out: Joan of Arc, whose "voices" led her king to coronation and herself to flames and sainthood, and the glittering Gilles de Rais, Marshal of France, whose dark voices led him to the scaffold and hundreds of little victims to a ghastly death. Joan is still a heroine to France; Gilles has become a symbol of limitless evil.

Gilles' story is told here through the eyes of Raoul de Saumur, his childhood companion and lifelong comrade-in-arms, impelled by curiosity to fathom his friend's secret, yet terrified himself by what he might discover.

"An historical meditation on the paralysing fascination of evil" – *The Times*.

"The novel has to cope with this ghoul and with the enigma of Joan herself and does so with a solid sense of period" – *Guardian*.

ISBN 0 85449 006 X (paperback only)

Tom Wakefield
THE DISCUS THROWERS

Considered by many critics to be one of Britain's most original contemporary writers, Tom Wakefield's *Mates* and *Drifters* have been widely praised for the way they depict the humour and pathos of human relationships. His latest novel continues in the same vein, charting the progress of five everyday figures who react against the social conventions that shackle their lives.

"Wakefield is an accomplished narrator; detached, witty and knowing" – *The Times*.

"It's refreshing to come across an English novelist who knows exactly what he's doing and does it resoundingly well" – Peter Ackroyd.

"Tom Wakefield is one of our most engaging of novelists" – Valentine Cunningham, *Times Literary Supplement*.

ISBN 0 907040 79 9 (paperback)
0 907040 80 2 (cloth)